D0124081

CANYONS

Also by Gary Paulsen

CANYONS

GARY
PAULSEN

**Delacorte
Press**

Published by
Delacorte Press
Bantam Doubleday Dell Publishing Group, Inc.
666 Fifth Avenue
New York, New York 10103

Copyright © 1990 by Gary Paulsen

All rights reserved. No part of this book may be reproduced or transmitted in any form or by any means, electronic or mechanical, including photocopying, recording or by any information storage and retrieval system, without the written permission of the Publisher, except where permitted by law.

The trademark Delacorte Press® is registered in the U.S. Patent and Trademark Office.

Library of Congress Cataloging in Publication Data

Paulsen, Gary.
    Canyons / by Gary Paulsen.
      p. cm.
    Summary: Finding a skull on a camping trip in the canyons outside El Paso, Texas, Brennan becomes involved with the fate of a young Apache Indian who lived in the late 1800s.
    ISBN 0-385-30153-7
    [1. Texas—Fiction. 2. Apache Indians—Fiction. 3. Indians of North America —Texas—Fiction.] I. Title.
PZ7.P2843Can   1990
[Fic]—dc20   90-2829
                                       CIP
                                       AC

designed by Logo Studios - B. Gold

Manufactured in the United States of America
September 1990
10 9 8 7 6 5 4 3 2 1
BVG

To Angenette
and James Wright—with deep gratitude,
true love, and gentle respect
for the joy
of their life

1
Quickening

Soon he would be a man.

Not after months, or years, as it had been, but in a day. In a day Coyote Runs would be a man and take the new name which only he would know because finally after fourteen summers they were taking him on a raid.

He had difficulty believing it. For this summer and two summers past he had gone time and time again to the old place, the medicine place, the ancient place in another canyon only he knew about, and prayed for manhood—all for nothing. For the whole of this summer and two summers past he had been ignored, thought of as still a boy.

And now it was upon him.

In the morning he had risen early and walked

away from the camp before the fires yet smoked and gone to the stream to rinse his mouth and take a cool drink and nothing seemed different.

He had gone to the ponies and looked at them and thought how it would be someday to own a pony, two of them, many of them, when he was a man and could go on raids to take horses and a Mexican saddle with silver on it like Magpie had done when he became a man and who could now walk with his neck swollen.

All someday. That's how he thought then, in the morning, it would all come someday. He would be an Apache warrior and ride down past the bluebellies' fort across the dirty little river into Mexico and prove that he was a man.

Someday.

After he had watched the pony herd for a time he walked back to the huts in the early morning sun and saw that his mother was making a fire to heat a pot of stew made from a fat steer they had taken from Carnigan's ranch. The rancher had many such steers and did not mind when the village took one. He liked to watch his mother make fire. She was round and her face shone in the sun and her hands were so sure when she piled the sticks and struck the white man's lucifer stick to make the fire that he thought of her as not just his mother but the mother of the fire. As she was the mother of the stew and the wood and the sand and the hut and Coyote Runs. The mother of all things.

Then Magpie had come out of his hut where he slept with his family though he was a man because he did not have his own wife yet. He saw Coyote Runs sitting near his mother and came to him and squatted next to him in the dirt.

"It is a fine morning," he said, which caused Coyote Runs to look at him because his voice was light and teasing. "A fine morning to be a man. . . ."

Coyote Runs said nothing but had a sour taste in his mouth. It was not like Magpie to make fun of him or to be proud so that it showed in a teasing voice.

"I have heard stories," Magpie said, and now Coyote Runs could tell that he was teasing openly. But he was smiling and his eyes were not mean.

"What kind of stories?"

"I have heard stories of a new raid to where the silver saddles are. A raid which will leave tomorrow. A raid which will have all the warriors on it."

Coyote Runs felt it now, the small excitement that came from surprises.

"All the warriors and men there are. Tell me, warrior, do you have a pony?"

"I'm going?" Coyote Runs tried to keep his voice even.

Magpie smiled wider and nodded. "It is thought that you could come to hold the horses and see how it is to be on a raid. Sancta said it, said you could come by name."

Coyote Runs thrilled inside but tried to remain cool, not show it, as was proper. For a man. As a man should act. Sancta was a scarred old man who could not be touched by arrows or bullets who had led all the raids since Coyote Runs knew there were raids; Sancta decided who would go and who would stay. And he had decided. "I do not have a proper pony for war but it is perhaps true that I have a friend with a pony." He looked pointedly at Magpie. "Do I have such a friend?"

Magpie nodded. "I will loan you that small brown pony with the white eye. Until you can get your own."

"Until I can get my own."

Magpie stood. "I think I will go down to the stream now and clean myself."

Coyote Runs nodded but did not stand. Inside he was ready to explode but he remained cool. "Yes. The water was good this morning."

And he thought I am to be a man. I am going on a raid and I am to be a man.

There was much to do. He must ready himself and his bow and check his arrows; he must make certain that everything was the best that it could be.

I am to be a man.

There was much to do.

2

Brennan Cole lived in El Paso, Texas, and each afternoon after school he ran. He did not run from anything and did not run to anything, did not run for track nor did he run to stay in shape and lose weight.

He ran to be with himself.

He was tall and thin and healthy with brown hair that grew thick and had to be cut often and because he ran in shorts with no shirt and wearing a headband instead of a cap and because El Paso sits at the base of Mount Franklin and burns in the hot sun for most of the year he was the color of rich, burnt leather.

He did not know his father. He lived alone with his mother and when he was home—which was less and less as he approached fifteen and his mother spent more and more time working to live, working to be, working to feed and clothe her only son—the two of them existed in a kind of quiet tolerance.

She did not dislike him so much as resent the burden she thought he was; and he did not dislike her so much as want to relieve her of the burden.

He was still too young for fast-food jobs but he mowed lawns for a lawn care service, working for an old man named Stoney Romero, who paid him in cash and did not ask questions nor give answers except to aim Brennan at yards with a mower. Brennan did not make much, but he fed himself and bought clothes for school and special shoes.

For his running, he thought now, turning on Yandell Street headed for the apartment over the house where he and his mother lived. I need money only for shoes for running.

It is all I need to do—to run is all there is. When I am running it is all, everything. Nothing matters. Not the father that I do not know or the mother that does not know me or the school that I hate or money or not money—all of that disappears when I run.

When I float. When I run and float. God, he thought, his legs felt like they belonged to somebody else, somebody who never became tired, and when he looked down at them pumping, driving, moving him forward they marveled him. From all the running, from the daily running in the streets and up the hills they had become so strong he didn't know them.

There was traffic but he keyed his steps and ran across the street at an angle, picking up speed as he passed in front of an army pickup from Fort Bliss. I can run for all of time, run forever.

It was May and very hot, close to ninety in the shade. But dry heat—always dry heat in the desert—and it didn't take him down. Nothing took him down.

Except being home.

There was that, he thought, turning up the block and seeing their apartment and his mother's old Volkswagen, knowing that he would not be able to be with himself any longer. Only home took him down.

She had company.

She belonged to one of those parents-without-husbands groups or whatever they were and from time to time she would bring different people around and he would have to meet them. He tried to be nice to them, but they always looked at him with open pity and he didn't feel that he should be pitied simply because he didn't know his father, had never met him, didn't know who he was, or any of the other ways they put it. The truth was he had never really had a father and so it didn't matter.

But she went to these meetings and she told everything about herself at the meetings, which included him, and everything about him, and so these people he didn't know knew all about him and would come to the house with her sometimes and sit and pity him.

They all wanted to "share," and "care," and "get in touch with their feelings," and on and on. The first few times they had come and met with his mother in their kitchen he had thought it might be all right and that his mother might get out of herself. But after a time, and many, many meetings, it just seemed that she was spending all her time messing with herself and not trying to really fix anything.

And I have to go in, he thought. I have to work for Stoney and that means I have to change clothes and get jeans on to go to work and that means I have to go inside. If it were not for that, he would run past the apartment and keep running for a half hour or so, until the company was gone.

Maybe if he just whipped in and changed, he could get away before he got nailed.

But it didn't work that way.

He ran up the back steps and into the kitchen, where his mother was sitting with a man.

He was pleasant enough. Tall, slightly heavy, with short hair.

"Brennan," his mother said, "I'd like you to meet Bill Halverson."

Brennan nodded. "Hi."

"Hi."

And that was it, or he thought it was. Brennan went into his room and changed quickly and threw on a T-shirt and made his way back outside to jog down to Stoney's place to ride in his old pickup out to mow lawns.

Later he would think back on this time; later when he had begun to try to find his spirit and see the dance of the sun, later when his life was torn to pieces and he was trying to make it whole again, he would look back on this moment, this exact moment when it started, and wonder how it could be.

How anything so big could come from something so small and simple.

"Hi."

"Hi."

And it changed his whole life.

3
Dust Spirits

Coyote Runs let the small brown pony pick its way down the side of a dry wash and thought that it was as his spirits, the spirits of the dust, had told him— everything was perfect.

The afternoon before they left on the ride south to Mexico he had gone to the ancient medicine place, the secret place, and had spoken to his spirits to ask for guidance and bravery to have a thick neck and be a man. He had waited for a long time and nothing came and he was beginning to worry that it was all wrong, that there would not be a sign, when it came:

Out below him to the east in a dry lake bed the wind swirled and picked up a column of dust and carried it heavenward, carried it to the spirits, carried his wishes high and away, as high and away as the hawk, as the dust, and he knew it would be all right. Would be perfect.

He painted the pony with one circle around one eye so that it could see well if they had to run at night and put tobacco on its hooves to make them fast, to show the spirits where he needed help.

Each arrow he placed tobacco on, using tobacco from a round metal tin that Magpie had found in an old shed at the Quaker school when the two of them had gone to the school to learn how it was to be white. They learned nothing except some symbols on a black stone written with a piece of white dirt; symbols that meant their names in white man's words that the Quaker lady taught them which did them no good because nobody else could read them. But Magpie found the round tin with the lid in the shed so it was not all for nothing.

He did not have a gun. Some of the men had guns and all the soldiers had guns but he did not have a gun and would have to use the bow and the arrows and when he had put tobacco on each arrow he did the same for the bow, each time asking for the dust spirits to make them fly, make them shoot in the proper manner.

All afternoon he prepared himself and when the men sat that night and talked of the raid outside one of the huts he stood to the rear and listened. He thought for a moment that Magpie had been teasing him because two of the men looked at him. But when they did not tell him to leave he knew that he was to go on the raid, that Magpie had been telling him the truth, and his heart was full of joy.

It was the first time he had heard them talk of a raid when he was not sneaking and he saw other boys who were still too young hiding round the back of the firelight in the dark and felt pride that he was at last allowed to be with the men. He listened carefully, quietly, with great courtesy and said nothing.

"We will take extra horses in case there is an injury and ride to that place on the river where the land cuts low so the bluebellies cannot see us cross when we go or when we come back," Sancta said. He was wrinkled and had scars from many battles. There was a line across his forehead which was said to have come from the long knife of a bluebelly who had tried to cut the top of his head off and let the light into his brains.

And the men grunted and nodded and smoked in silence, spitting on the fire from time to time.

"We will stay tight in together until we get to that place below the cut on the river where the Mexican ranchers keep that big herd of horses for selling to the bluebellies."

More grunts and nods.

"There we will leave Coyote Runs with the extra horses and hit the herd and take as many horses as we can get running."

Now there were open exclamations and Coyote Runs felt a thrill of pride that he had been named by name as going on the raid. He turned to see if any of the hiding boys had heard but he could not see their faces, just shapes in the brush and darkness.

It did not matter, he thought then and thought now as his pony followed the rest of the men and extra horses. All that mattered was that the dust spirits were with him and had heard his request and that he was on the raid.

It would take three days riding out and around to get to the river that the white men used as a boundary and part of another day to ride south to where the Mexicans kept the big herd of horses and then two days to ride back driving the horses ahead of them. Six days, Coyote Runs thought, riding easily.

Six days to test himself and prove he was a man.

Surely there would be many ways for him to be a man in a week.

He used his heels to goad the brown pony up and out of a gully Sancta had led them to; ahead Magpie caught the sun and his long black hair shone like a raven's wing in the light and Coyote Runs smiled at the beauty of it.

Six whole days, Coyote Runs repeated. Six days to be a man.

4

"You must come in closer on the flower beds or there is too much for me to use the string on."

Stoney Romero gave him instructions the way he did all his other talking—his voice like gravel rattling around in a garbage can. He smoked cigarettes which he rolled from tobacco in a small plastic bag he carried because "tailormades" cost too much and he spent most of his time coughing and hacking.

"If the mower gets too close I'll take out the beds," Brennan explained. "And then you'll get chewed out and I'll get chewed out."

"Nobody chews me out," Stoney told him, and it was true. Brennan had never seen anybody speak crossly to the old man. Perhaps because he was scarred across his cheeks. A part-time worker also named Romero had told Brennan that it was from a knife fight in prison where Romero killed a man, but the part-time worker also told him that Fig New-ton cookies could cure baldness, so Brennan nodded. "I'll work in closer."

"As I said."

Stoney turned away and Brennan started the riding mower and began to mow. He liked the work, liked the way the mower worked in rows and cut even, fresh green lines with each round. Stoney had many lawns to mow for the people he called "the rich ones."

It wasn't even that they were all rich, although they did some lawns on houses that were huge old estates where there were statues around the pools and steel gates that had to be opened electrically. Many of the lawns belonged to army families who did not make as much money as Stoney. But they were all "the rich ones" to him, said with a sharpness to it that meant he did not respect them, and Brennan was glad for the work.

He needed the money. His mother had told him she couldn't afford to help him with his school clothes as much as she'd thought she would because she didn't get a raise she thought she would get. Brennan had tried to get other jobs but he was too young. They didn't care if he could do the work or not. He was too young.

And Stoney hadn't even asked about his age.

"Can you mow a lawn?" he'd asked, taking a deep drag on the small brown cigarette and coughing.

"Yes."

"You're hired. I will pay you three dollars an hour in cash at the end of each day and if you do not show up for work you are fired."

And he had been as good as his word. Usually work was almost impossible to find because of the closeness to Mexico—Juárez was right across the river—and the poverty there which sent thousands north each day to find work.

But Stoney had hired him and he'd worked now for almost all of June and July and Stoney had been as good as his word. Each day he paid Brennan in wrinkled bills and quarters and dimes and nickels, exactly the amount for the hours he had worked and each day Brennan went home and put the money in a jar in the cupboard.

It was adding up, the money.

Because I don't do anything, he thought, moving the mower in closer to the flower beds as instructed, squinting up at the hot sun and the Franklin Mountains that rose above the city—except work and sleep.

He had no really close friends, no girl—just himself. It was strange but he didn't seem to make connections with other kids. Last year for most of the year he'd been close to a boy named Carl and he guessed Carl had been his best friend. But Carl didn't run and Brennan did and after a time they just drifted apart and sort of stopped calling each other and that was that.

Some of the jocks wanted him to join the track team, as did the coach, Mr. Townsend. But they ran for the wrong reasons as far as Brennan was concerned. They ran to win, to be somebody, to get popular, to get girls, to get a letter—not just to run. Brennan ran for the joy of running, and to be with himself, and when he told the coach that, Mr. Townsend had looked at him as if he were crazy.

"You're good," the coach had said, "really good. You could help the school, make something of yourself, be popular. . . ."

But Brennan could not see why it was important to do those things and when the coach saw that he only wanted to run and when the jocks saw that he only wanted to run and the other kids saw that he only wanted to run they left him alone.

To run.

He worked in close around the flowers. Stoney was right, he could get closer. But it was dangerous and if he took out a flower bed, or even cut the edge off one they would probably lose the job. And he might lose his job as well.

So he worked slowly and carefully and the afternoon went slowly. They finished the lawn with the flower beds, then another one which wasn't too far away and then they loaded into Stoney's old pickup to drive to a third one, which would be the last for the afternoon.

On the way, out of nowhere, Stoney decided to talk to him.

"Kid."

Brennan looked at him. Generally, other than giving instructions, Stoney treated Brennan as if he weren't there.

Just sat smoking and scratching or working by himself and left Brennan alone to his own thoughts.

Brennan looked across the truck at him. "What?"

"Ever think how stupid this is?"

"What?"

"This whole thing with the lawns. Here we are in the middle of a desert where nothing grows but mesquite and cactus and some snakes and people spend all their money on water just to get grass to grow so they can spend even *more* money to get us to cut it for them so they can spend even *more* money on water to get it to grow again so we can cut it. . . . Isn't it stupid?"

"Well, I guess so. But a lawn is nice. A green one."

"What does your old man do?"

The question came fast, dropped out of nowhere, but Brennan had answered it so many times, the answer was always ready. "Nothing. He died when I was a baby."

The lie. It came so easy now and he had done it so many times that he almost believed it himself. He died when I was a baby. It was so sad. He died when I was a baby.

The truth was, he had run off with another woman when Brennan was three and Brennan could only just remember a faint image of how he had looked—like an old photograph blurred and faded with age. For a time he had hated his father for leaving, but even that was gone. Now there was nothing.

"Tough." Stoney coughed and spit out the window. "Having no father . . ."

"It's not so bad," Brennan said quickly, too quickly. "Mom and I get along."

"Well, hell, it might have been worse the other way. My old man lived and spent all his time sucking on a tequila bottle and beating the snot out of me. There were a few times I wished he would die, come to think of it. Maybe if your old man had lived he would have beat you."

Brennan didn't answer, sat looking out the window. The heat coming down from the mountains, the sky, up from the asphalt, was like a blast furnace. It made the metal on the truck door so hot that if he moved his arm to a new place it burned him. But he liked the heat just the same. There was something clean about it, fresh. Yeah, he thought, if he'd lived he probably would have beat me. But even that might have been better than what they had now. Now it was so . . . so nothing. He and his mother just spent all their time in the house getting along. Just a day and then another day and then another getting along.

And her friends, of course. There were her friends.

Like this guy Bill.

He wondered if that would turn into another relationship. His mother had gone through so many relationships, he had lost count. Dozens. Well, maybe not dozens. But many.

Some of them had moved in and he had played the game with them. Treated them like substitute fathers. But he no longer did that. He was too old for it and it just felt silly. Most of them had been good to him, some very good. One named Frank who showered him with presents and toys and candy and took him places and was almost sticky about it. But even with Frank he had trouble thinking of him as a father. It wasn't the same as having a real one. Or at least that's how he thought.

They unloaded the mowers and mowed the last lawn. It was large and they finished in the evening, just before dusk.

"You want a burger?" Stoney asked while he paid Brennan. It sounded like an invitation but Brennan knew that what it meant was that Stoney would take him by a McDonald's where he could buy his own burger and eat it on the way home in the truck. Brennan shook his head.

"No. I'd better get home. Mom is waiting." Which wasn't true but served as well as the truth and Stoney nodded and drove him home in silence.

Brennan saw that his mother's car was still parked in front of the house, along with another car he had seen earlier that day and when he walked in he saw Bill sitting at the kitchen table with his mother.

"Oh, Bren," his mother said, her eyes wide and smiling. "Come on in here. We've got great news. We're going camping with Bill. . . ."

Oh great, Brennan thought, another relationship.

5
Nightride

The village lay east of the white man's town of Alamogordo three, four days riding but they did not ride toward that place. Coyote Runs knew there was nothing in that place but dusty little houses and a place where men drank until they fell down and puked. He had been there once when he had been going to the school with the Quaker lady and was sickened by what he had seen.

The raiding party would not go near Alamogordo because they might be seen. Instead they rode straight south over the tops of the wild canyons that fed out into the great desert and the place with the white sand the Mexicans called Jornada del Meurto—the journey of death. It was said that a Spanish warrior in a time long ago before there were even horses except for those he brought rode through that place and lost many men and had to eat some horses but Coyote Runs did not believe all of that.

There were many stories of hard journeys told by old people, some of their own stories and some they'd heard from the Mexicans, but he did not find them all truthful. He had eaten horse himself many times and it was not so special a thing to do; the meat was good and the fat was yellow. If there was fat. But it was a silliness, a stupid thing to do—eating a horse. There were better things to eat and you would not lose your ride.

Coyote Runs shook his head. All this thinking was a waste. It was just that it was truly dark now and Sancta continued the ride, letting the horses pick the trail as they made their way south. There was nothing to see and Coyote Runs rode in silence, as did Magpie in front of him and all the others, and without anything to see or anybody to speak to or listen to his thoughts went a way of their own.

Like thinking of the place of white sands. He had been to it only once though he could see it from the medicine place and thought it looked like the snow that covered the mountains in the winter but when he touched it the sand was hot. White with the sun and hot. Like hot snow. Could there be such a thing, he wondered—such a thing as hot snow?

His pony stumbled and he grabbed its mane to

pull it upright. Some horses could see better in the dark than others and he hoped that Sancta's horse was one of the good ones or they could all ride off a cliff. There were many steep drops to the right and he knew that if he could see it would be possible to see across the desert to the other range of mountains, the jagged-tooth mountains that the white men called the Organ Mountains because it reminded them somehow of the music box the Quaker lady had in her home that required you to pump your feet to make the music come out the pipes. The music had been nice, but naming the mountains after the box made no sense at all to Coyote Runs. That mountains could look like the small box, mountains that reached to the sky with arms of stone, could make the white men think of the small squeaky box in the Quaker lady's home was a silliness.

He shook his head again. About as much a silliness as riding along in the darkness on his first raiding party thinking small thoughts when he should be thinking of becoming a man.

He must think of that as he rode. Becoming a man. He must ride straight and think of serious things, think of the raid and not being afraid if he was called upon to do battle or if they met the bluebellies.

He straightened and tried to see ahead in the darkness, tried to pay close attention to where he thought Magpie was moving ahead of him.

He must be serious, as serious as a man must be.

6

Brennan looked out the window of the van and worked very hard at not being angry. They were driving north of El Paso on the highway that went through the desert up to Alamogordo and he sat looking sideways out at the huge rock canyons that led up from the desert into the mountains. They were beautiful, colored layers of rock and natural formations that looked painted and yet he was having trouble seeing any of the beauty in them.

He'd somehow gotten cornered on this camping trip thing and he was still trying to figure out how it had happened.

Normally he was really good at avoiding becoming involved in his mother's business. When she got into aerobics he avoided it and when she did the health food he avoided it and once he'd even avoided it when she was going with a jock who thought he knew all about running and actually spent time running with Brennan, running alongside him when he ran, telling him how to hold his arms and move his legs and how to breathe. That time Brennan had outrun him —just hung a right and headed up toward the drive around Mount Franklin, loping along and letting the guy fall back until he was just a speck.

But sometimes you lose, he thought, looking at the scenery blur by—sometimes no matter what you do you lose.

And this was one of those times.

Two days, no, three days ago he'd been standing in the kitchen and his mother had been smiling and saying:

"We're going camping with Bill and his youth group."

And his mind had raced through a thousand excuses, some new, some old. She had started going to this new church and she'd met Bill at a church dinner and Bill was active with a youth group—she had explained it later to Brennan, her cheeks glowing. But he hadn't known that at the moment, at the second, the instant when he thought of all the excuses. I'm busy, I have to work, Stoney has a lot of new lawns—the cards flipped through in his mind and he opened his mouth to use one of them but there was such a hopeful look in his mother's eyes, such a childlike hopeful look that the words that came out had nothing to do with what he was thinking:

"Oh? That will be nice."

Dead, he thought looking out the window of the van. I was dead when I opened my mouth.

And once he'd said that he couldn't get out of it. Not really. And his mother *had* wanted it so badly, or seemed to.

And he'd thought, oh well, it won't be so bad. Overnight out in the desert with Bill and his mother and some kids from Bill's church youth group. How bad could it be?

He almost smiled now, thinking back on it, would have smiled except that it *had* turned out so awful. The kids —there were seven of them, all boys, all about eight years old—were monsters. They were all over the van like gremlins, wouldn't let themselves be buckled in, and with Bill and Brennan's mother in the front seat and Brennan in the back with the kids—he thought of them as the pack—the main load of work with the children dropped on Brennan.

It was like being in a nest of rats. They climbed on the seats, bit each other, fought, and wouldn't do anything Brennan told them to do. One of them, a boy named Ralph Beecher, just sat in the corner of the backseat kicking anybody who came within range.

By the time they were out of El Paso, Brennan knew he was in trouble and within twenty miles of the highway heading north he had his hands full. He tried holding them down, pushing them away, scowling, swearing at them— nothing worked and finally he turned away and ignored them, stared out the window and wished he were anywhere else.

Bill was nice enough, and that was the problem, really. He was too nice. He didn't bother to say anything to the kids and they took that for permission to do anything they wanted to do—which stopped just short of unscrewing each other's heads.

When they had driven fifty or sixty miles Bill suddenly slowed the van and took a narrow, winding road that led off east into the desert, toward the canyons.

It did not look like they were going toward any kind of campground, Brennan thought, looking over his mother's shoulder out the front window of the van. The road grew worse and worse and at last they were winding over rocks and sand and through sand dunes on little more than a narrow trail. Eventually even that ended.

"Now," Bill said, getting out and stretching, "we walk."

"Walk?"

Brennan couldn't help himself, his voice had a definite down tone to it and his mother shot him a warning look. Walk—with these kids? Brennan got out of the van and shook his head, you'd have to have a whip and a chair.

But if Bill heard his voice he gave no indication. He took gear from the rack on top of the van, laughing and talking and pointing.

"See that canyon?"

Over them rose the rock canyons leading up to the mountains. They had driven past several of them on the highway and turned into the fourth or fifth one. Brennan couldn't tell for sure now that they were so close to the bluff wall.

"It's called Horse Canyon. I came up here once years ago hiking and found a trail to a spring in the back of it. That's where we're going, back up in the canyon and camp by the spring."

Brennan looked up at the canyon. It seemed to be all rocks and cliffs—he could see no evidence of any kind of trail at all. The bed of the canyon, which lay straight before them, seemed to be an old riverbed filled with enormous boulders. It was impassable. To get "back up in" the canyon it would be necessary to work along the river and Brennan couldn't see a way to do it.

"I don't see a trail," he said, trying to keep his voice light. He still did not want to ruin this for his mother.

"Don't worry. There's one there," Bill said. He gave each boy a sleeping bag to carry and shouldered a pack, motioned Brennan to take another pack and Brennan's mother to pick up the rolled-up tents. "Really, it's not hard at all."

Which was not quite accurate.

It was true that it wasn't impossible, as Brennan had thought, but it was hard enough so that Brennan had to help some of the smaller children in a few of the places—just to climb over boulders and cuts across the trail—and even Brennan's mother felt it was a bit much.

"Do we have to go all the way to the rear of the canyon?" she asked at one point.

"Aren't there some nice places, you know, closer?"

But Bill insisted. They worked their way up on a small trail that led along the dry riverbed filled with boulders and smooth, dishlike bowls made by an ancient river that had roared down the canyon. In some places newer runoff had cut across what little trail there was, carrying it down into the riverbed, and here they had to drop into the cuts and climb out the other side.

Whatever else he is or isn't, Brennan thought, watching Bill up ahead with the pack on his back and helping the small boys—he isn't a wimp. Brennan was in good shape from running and he was soon breathing hard and his mother, who did not run or exercise very much, was almost staggering.

It was the sort of place Brennan would have loved, had he not been with the rat pack, as he thought of them by this time. The canyon walls rose straight up into the late afternoon sky; towering red and yellow with dark streaks, one bluff feeding to another up into the mountains. To say it was beautiful, he thought, seeing them shoot up over him, was just not enough. The beauty seemed to come almost from inside his mind, so that he saw the cliffs and canyon walls as if he had almost painted them. Here and there a scraggly pine hung on to life and yucca plants and cactus in bloom made color spots that seemed to make the cliffs even more striking. Art, he thought—it was like art. The year before, he'd taken an art appreciation class—largely because he had to—and the teacher, a short woman named Mrs. Dixon, had spent many periods trying to get them to see the art.

"See it," she would say to them, holding up a picture of a painting by Rembrandt or van Gogh or Whistler. "Really *see* it, inside it—see the brushstrokes? See what the artist was trying to do?"

And he tried that now, to really *see* the canyon, see what the artist was trying to do with it.

God, he thought—that was the artist. What was God trying with this?

Except that he was seeing the beauty with one eye while he was trying to watch ahead with the other and keep up with Bill and his mother and the kids, who were all over the place, sticking their fingers in cactus and screaming, throwing rocks down into the riverbed to hear them bounce, spitting off of boulders, hitting each other, jerking their pants down and mooning each other, throwing rocks at each other . . .

It was hard to see the beauty.

It took them almost two hours, until evening, to get up into a point where the canyon seemed to flatten out a bit and then another half hour of walking to get across a grassy area to a place where a trail dropped down into some small cottonwoods that were growing around a tiny pool of green, clear water.

"Oh," Brennan's mother said. "Isn't it pretty here?"

Bill turned and smiled at them. "It's like a calendar picture, isn't it?"

And it was almost sweet. Even the monsters stopped and were quiet for a moment or two. In the sudden silence Brennan heard birds singing and felt the sun on his neck. It had been hot but there was a coolness in the evening air that felt refreshing. Brennan lowered his pack and sleeping bag and two other bags and packs he'd been carrying for the younger boys.

"Is this it?" he asked, looking up and around. They were in the end of a box canyon and the walls rose above them making a huge amphitheater. The kids had been yelling and whistling for half an hour, listening to the echoes, but in their silence Brennan could hear himself breathe.

Without knowing quite why, he held his breath.

And in that instant something about the place took him, came into him and held his thoughts. Something he couldn't understand. Some pull, some reaching and pulling thing that made the hair stand up on the back of his neck.

He looked to see if any of the others felt it but they didn't seem to. Bill was still holding his arms out and smiling, the kids were beginning to move again, and his mother was in the act of dropping her pack on the ground and blowing hair out of her eyes.

He let his eyes move up and around the canyon again but could see nothing out of the ordinary. The rock cliffs towered over them, blocking the sun off so that now though it was still light they were in shade and it became almost cool.

Birds flew across the canyon. High overhead an eagle caught a thermal and wheeled out of sight past the edge of the canyon wall.

He shook his head. Strange, the feeling, he'd never had it before and now it was gone. Somebody was saying something and he looked down and saw Bill nodding.

"Yes. This is where we spend the night, where we camp. Let's get wood for a fire and make some dinner. I'm sure everyone is starved, aren't we, boys?"

The monsters started screaming and running in circles grabbing sticks and Brennan had to fight to keep from yelling at them.

It was going to be a long, looong night.

7
Visions

He did well.

During the night they went past a camp of bluebellies who had stopped on one of their patrols and Coyote Runs did well.

There were only eight of the bluebellies and they had a large fire as they always did to keep away the darkness so it was easy to see them and count them and would have been easy to kill them but Sancta shook his head.

Not this time. They stood for a time not a long bowshot from the soldiers and their fire, pinching their horses' muzzles so they would not make sounds to the soldiers' horses, so close the glow from the fire lit their faces, and could have gone in amongst them. Coyote Runs had his bow ready, an arrow on the string, and knew he could hit one and maybe another soldier as they rode in, knew it in his heart but Sancta said no.

Shaking his head once, a jerk from side to side that they could not miss and the old leader turned and led his horse back into the night.

And Coyote Runs brought his pony around and led it silently in back of Magpie and did not shoot an arrow at the camp, as he wished, but held back though his neck was stiff and swollen with the need to go amongst the soldiers.

They rode all night. There were no watering places for the horses but they had carried water in clay pots tied to their horses' blankets and stopped to walk and moisten the horses' mouths to keep them moving.

Twice Coyote Runs' pony seemed about to go down and he filled his mouth with water and spit it down the horse's throat so it would not waste out the side of the horse's mouth and the pony kept moving and he thought:

I am doing it. I am doing well. I am a man.

They rode all that night until the ridge led to a flat place with dead grass that seemed to go forever and here they stopped and made a cold camp.

They did not stay more than three hours, enough to let the horses rest but not so long they would stiffen up, then Sancta started walking again, leading his mount, and they all followed him.

Always south.

Sancta trotted ahead of them like a hurrying bear and after a time Coyote Runs realized he was beginning to see things. There was gray light coming from the east, over his left shoulder, the beginning of the new day.

Ahead he saw Sancta rolling along, his shoulders moving from side to side, his knee-high moccasins kicking up dust as he ran, his long black hair swaying from side to side and Coyote Runs knew he looked the same.

Knew that he could run this way all day, all night, as long as Sancta would need him to run.

Off to the right, many miles away, he could see the mountains that stood over the place the Mexicans called El Paso del Norte—the pass of the north—where the town lay, the white town and more, the fort where the bluebellies lived, Fort Bliss. That was there as well.

Coyote Runs had never been south this way and so had never seen the fort but he had heard about it. Buildings made of dirt as the Pueblos and Mexicans made them, arranged in a square for protection.

As if, he thought, as if the Apache would come against them in the fort. As if they would simply ride in against them in the fort and die.

Ho! There was madness there. In the bluebellies. The same as they wore dark wool clothes in the summer, buttoned tight to the collar so the heat could not get away and heavy hats to keep the heat in their heads and rode their horses through the heat of the day—all crazy.

But they fought well. He had never fought them but he heard stories, from Sancta and the others, sitting around the fire—stories of their fights with the bluebellies. They were not easy to kill.

It was hard light now, the sun showing, and he could tell that Sancta was looking for something as he ran, leading his horse.

In moments he swung off to the left and brought the party to the edge of a depression in the desert, a low gully surrounded by mesquite that hung out over the edges. It was as far across as Coyote Runs could throw a rock and Sancta led them down into the bottom of it.

"For the day," he said to them. "We stop here. Where we can't be seen by the bluebelly patrols. Sleep."

Coyote Runs led his pony beneath an overhang of mesquite so there was some small shade and lay on his back on the sand with the rein to the bridle tightly wrapped around his hand.

Magpie settled in next to him so the two horses stood closely together and could use their tails to switch flies from one another.

"Well, how do you like your first raid so far?" he asked.

But Coyote Runs was already asleep.

8

Brennan had thought as soon as it was dark the children would settle down, or at least slow a bit in their behavior.

He was wrong.

If anything they became more hyper and while Bill —Brennan was starting to think perhaps he wasn't really aware of things, like the world around him—while Bill took it well and no matter what they did seemed largely to ignore any of the problems, Brennan quickly became sick of them.

Short of tying them down—and he wished he'd brought rope—he couldn't control them at all. They were in his pack, in his bag where he'd spread it by the fire pit, throwing his gear around.

But after a time he noticed that as darkness came into the canyon, dropping like a black sheet down over them, the boys stayed more in the area of the fire. They didn't act afraid, but they didn't want to leave the glow of the fire either and that gave Brennan an idea.

He moved his sleeping bag farther and farther from the fire until he was nestled beneath a large boulder sticking up out of the ground, back under the overhang. There was a small sheltered area here, only large enough for one bag, and he spread it out on the dried grass and began to make himself comfortable.

"What are you doing?"

His mother had walked up in back of him while he was spreading his bag.

"Don't you want to be around the fire?"

"Mom . . ." He started to say something about the kids but let it go. She was so happy, or seemed to be happy with this Bill character, that he didn't want to do anything to ruin it for her. "This just looked like a neat place to set up."

She nodded—the glow from the fire lighted her cheek and it looked golden. Something about her face looked young, very young. "I know why you're up here—they're horrible, aren't they?"

"God," he said. "Like animals."

"Maybe they'll sleep pretty soon."

Brennan smiled. "Not unless you drive wooden stakes through their hearts. . . ."

She laughed and he'd somehow never felt closer to her. "But he's nice, isn't he? Bill, I mean."

Brennan nodded. "Yes. He is. I can't believe what he takes from them and never gets mad."

"I like him. A lot."

"That's nice—really."

"A lot."

She turned and walked back to the fire and he watched her go and felt a kind of sadness. There had been others that she had liked. A lot. And they somehow all came to nothing and she wanted somebody so badly, needed someone so badly that Brennan almost wept for her sometimes.

He rose from the bag and moved toward the fire. What the heck, maybe if he took the kids for a while Bill and his mother would get a little time to know each other. What would it hurt?

He sat by the fire. "Who knows a story?"

And it worked. They all settled in around him, sitting by the fire in the yellow glow, their faces looking up at him. It couldn't be, he thought, it couldn't be the same group of wild things that just a few minutes ago were tearing each other apart.

"I said," he repeated, "who knows a story?"

They all looked at each other and shook their heads. None of them knew a story.

Bill and Brennan's mother sat next to each other across the fire from Brennan. Bill coughed.

"I know a story," he said, "or not a story so much as some information about these canyons."

Brennan could see that it wasn't exactly what the kids were expecting, but they held still and waited.

"There are four or five of these canyons along this big ridge," Bill said, pointing up over his shoulder where the cliffs rose into the mountains. "And some called it the last stronghold of the Apache nation."

That got them. It also got Brennan. "What do you mean?"

"I'm kind of fuzzy on it, but north of here there is a canyon called Dog Canyon that also has a spring in it. I guess the Apaches would raid down south and then run back to these canyons to hide and the army would come after them."

"Were there battles?" one of the small kids asked. "With shooting and blood and guts and stuff?"

Bill nodded.

"All *right*!"

"There were several fights in Dog Canyon and there might have been some others in this canyon, in all the canyons along this ridge line. Soldiers and Apaches were both killed and . . ." here he paused and looked at Brennan and hid a wink ". . . they say that in the night sometimes you can hear the sounds of battle and that the ghosts of the dead warriors and soldiers walk in the darkness."

He stopped talking and there was silence around the fire. Far away a nightbird called and the sound seemed almost human—close enough so the boys drew together.

"I don't think I would run around too much at

night," Brennan said, taking advantage of the situation. "You know, out away from the fire."

But he hadn't needed to say it. Two of the boys, a set of twins named Glockens, said they weren't afraid of any old ghosts but they didn't stray more than ten feet from the fire and were very happy to toast marshmallows and drink hot chocolate made by Brennan's mother and Bill.

Bill told some more stories—plain ghost stories—and the children sat still, listening, and finally it was time for bed.

Brennan nodded good night to his mother and Bill and headed up to his bed beneath the rock, carrying a cup of hot chocolate. There was a light dew condensing on his bag and he shook it off before crawling inside. Then he sat up, the bag around him, and looked down at the fire below as the rest of the group crawled inside their bags, sipping his hot chocolate.

It wasn't so bad, this trip, he thought. The kids had finally settled down and his mother was right, Bill was a good guy. He hoped well for his mother.

The fire died quickly and he could hear the kids mumbling and talking for a short time, then it was quiet and still he sat.

He felt strange. The chocolate grew cold in his hand and he sat and let the canyon come in around him. There was no moon, but enough light came from the stars so that when his eyes grew used to the darkness he could see the canyon walls moving up into the sky.

Somewhere far away something screamed a faint cry

—almost like a woman or child screaming—and he started, then remembered reading somewhere that mountain lions screamed that way and thought it must be a cougar somewhere way off. There were mountains and more mountains up over the ridges and there must be mountain lions up there in the peaks.

I have lived so close to this, he thought, and never been here, never seen this beautiful place. He had been in the mountains close to El Paso but they were dry, dead, hot and baked airless peaks—not like this. Not with cool breezes and springs and cottonwoods and birds and lions, if it was a lion. He wondered for a moment if he should be frightened of the lion, then decided against it. From what he'd read they didn't bother people at all and it must have been miles away. The sleepers below him hadn't even heard it.

He put the cup down and lay back but still sleep wouldn't come.

Something was there, some strange thing that bothered him. He had felt it before when they first came into the end of the canyon and it was still there, the feeling. He couldn't shake it.

An unease, a restlessness that wouldn't go away. He closed his eyes and thought of things to make him sleep, boring things, but even that didn't work. In the end he sat up again, staring out across the canyons over the sleepers below him, a strange uneasiness in his heart that would not go away.

And the night came down.

9
The Raid

Oh yes, it had been something, the raid, Coyote Runs thought, holding tight to the pony with his legs. It had been a thing to see.

They had ridden through part of the night, spitting water into their horses' mouths until they arrived at the river where the horses could drink, just at dawn, and had found the large horse herd before the sun had risen completely above the line of land to the east.

Sancta had motioned to Coyote Runs to ride up to him and he had done so.

"Stay here with the extra horses. We will ride amongst them and take many horses and come back this way. Let us go by, then come in at the rear of the herd to help move them."

Coyote Runs wanted to shake his head, wanted

to say that he wished to ride amongst the Mexicans who were watching the horses to prove that he was a man, ride amongst them and fight but he did not. Sancta had given an order and that was the way things would be.

But he could see the horse herd, or part of it. Sancta and the others left him on the back side of a small rise but as soon as they rode off toward the Mexicans Coyote Runs moved forward and up onto the rise slightly so he could see some of it.

There were so many horses that they stretched as far as he could see into the mesquite and gullies. Many, most of them, were large and brown, as the bluebellies liked them, but many were of other colors and Coyote Runs saw a large horse the color of straw that he would have liked to take for his own. Indeed, his hands moved on the reins of the pony and his knees closed before he remembered that he must stay.

He saw one Mexican rider, a tiny figure on the other side of the herd, but the rider did not see him and in any event it made no difference. At that moment when he saw the Mexican rider there was a commotion to the right and a group of horses that had been down in a low swale suddenly broke into a run, heading straight for the river.

For a moment Coyote Runs could see no Apaches, then he saw heads above the dust and knew that Sancta and the others had cut the smaller herd away from the main body and were bringing them north.

They were not coming straight toward him but off to the side a bit, so he yelled and slapped the horses around him to get them moving to meet the others.

Dust and noise were everywhere. There was little wind in the morning, so when the horses raised dust it simply hung where it came up, and was added to by other dust until it was impossible to see anything and the hooves of the running horses—Coyote Runs thought that Sancta and the others must have cut out over a hundred of them—were like thunder.

Coyote Runs was confused for a time and actually drove the waiting horses that he was in charge of the wrong way, headed them south. In the dirt and noise it was easy to be wrong.

And there he could have died, he found, because he rode straight into a group of four Mexican riders. His small herd turned and started north, going right around him, as if sensing they were going the wrong way when they saw the Mexican vaqueros.

It was impossible to tell who was more surprised. He pulled his pony up, staring at them, and they pulled up, staring at him. Then two of them started shooting at him with their horse pistols that made clouds of smoke to mix with the dust and he wheeled his brown pony and followed the herd back to the north.

There was no sense to anything.

Because he had initially wound up going the wrong way, when he started back to the north he found himself to the rear of the main body of Mexican riders who were chasing Sancta and the others toward the river.

He did not know this at once, but suddenly found himself riding next to a Mexican man who looked sideways at him, drew a pistol from his belt, and aimed at Coyote Runs and shot.

Coyote Runs winced, waiting for the bullet to take him, but the Mexican did not aim well and it went wide and he veered away in the dirt clouds.

He passed others, driving the extra mounts north, passed two more and then three, all riding hard after Sancta but none of them shot at him and he thought he must have been given special power, special medicine to go through them like smoke so they could not see him, though he rode right next to them and had horses in front of him.

Suddenly he found himself running in water, the little pony almost going down when it hit the river. It was impossible to see anything, to know anything, and he merely hung on and hoped he would make it across the river.

Still noise, the pounding of hooves, and dust, even over the water dust that blew off the banks, but he believed in himself now, and his new medicine, so he drummed his heels into the brown pony and screamed at the horses in front of him and drove them across the water and up the bank and kept driving them.

North.

If he kept pushing them north he would catch up to Sancta and the others.

So he followed the dust and knew that he was a man now, knew that he was a man with large medicine who had passed the test, for had the Mexican not shot at him, shot directly where he was and the bullet had not hit him? And he had not been afraid. He had tightened his stomach to take the bullet, had waited for the shock of it, but had not been afraid and was not afraid now.

He drove them, slapping at the horses with the end of his bridle rope, keeping them driving in an easy lope ahead of him, following the dust for a mile, then another mile, and was on the edge of wondering if he would ever see the others when he ran into Magpie.

Who was aiming his old buffalo shooting rifle at him.

"Wait!" Coyote Runs said, pulling up. "It is me."

Magpie lowered the rifle and smiled. His face was so covered with dust that it seemed to crack when his lips moved. "Sancta heard hooves back here and thought it was some Mexicans still riding after us and sent me back to slow them down. It is lucky you called. I had begun to tighten the trigger."

It would not have mattered, Coyote Runs thought, because the bullet would not have been able to get through my new medicine, the medicine that protects me, but he said nothing.

"How far are they ahead?" he asked. He must look as Magpie did, with dust thick on his face and sweat streaks cutting through it, but the band of red cloth around his head kept the sweat from his eyes.

"They are by now another mile," Magpie said. "Come, let us catch up to them before some more Mexicans really do come and we are forced to fight and kill many of them and make their women sad."

Magpie swung in beside Coyote Runs and they pushed the spare horses into a run again, although not as hard as before. They did not really think the Mexicans would come because they did not like to ride across the river where they might run into the bluebellies. It was a fact that at times the bluebellies did not care what they shot as long as they shot something and the Mexicans did not like to face them.

They rode that way for a mile, then another half a mile, eating the dust from the horses Sancta and the others had taken, riding in silence as they pushed the horses ahead of them.

They caught up as Sancta was pushing the main herd of stolen horses across a dry lake. A small wind had come up and the dust blew away so Coyote Runs could see the horses ahead and below on the lake and he drew in his breath.

Such a herd he had never seen or thought to see. The village normally had a herd of thirty or forty horses, which included all the horses of all the men, but Sancta and the others were pushing well over a hundred horses ahead of them. Enormous wealth.

It was a great raid, a raid they would speak of for years around the fire and he, Coyote Runs, was part of it.

And now a man.

Magpie looked at him and made a sound in his throat, an almost growl of pride and exultation, and Coyote Runs matched the sound with one of his own.

"We have ridden amongst them," Magpie cried, his voice raw and low from the dust, "and taken many horses! We are the ones, we are the ones!"

They rode off down into the lake bed after Sancta and the rest of the men and horses with wild cries. Even the ponies seemed to have caught the excitement and Coyote Runs had to hold back on the rope to his pony's halter to keep him from running himself out.

They caught up with the main herd at the edge of the lake and there was much laughing and joking.

Not a man nor a horse had been hit, though the Mexicans had fired many shots at them, and Coyote Runs thought it must be that his medicine was so strong it had extended to cover all of them.

Truly, he thought, truly my medicine is strong and he wondered how that could be since he was so young. Most strong medicine went to older men. When they got back he would have to ask his mother about his medicine dream, his name dream. Was it stronger than other men dreamed? He had never heard such a thing. But his mother knew of dreams and visions and would be able to tell him.

Magpie and Coyote Runs put their small herd in with the main herd and they all started north. The men were positioned all around the horses, with Magpie and Coyote Runs bringing up the rear since they were the youngest and as such would get the least favored position. There was even more dust and dirt than before and soon Magpie untied his headband and tied it around his nose and mouth to filter out some of the dust.

Coyote Runs did the same and they rode that way all of the day without a single stop, until close to dark, when Sancta called a halt to rest the horses and change mounts.

They did not build fires.

"There may be riders coming after us," Sancta said, "although I do not think so. It will be better not to give them fires for guidance. Drink only a small amount of water and spit some into your horse's mouth. Take a Mexican horse for a new mount, they are still fresh."

Coyote Runs had his eye on a small reddish

horse and was making for it when he saw a flash of color out of the corner of his eye and turned to see the straw-colored horse standing sideways to him. It must have broken from the rest back before the river and come on its own.

He was the youngest and had to wait for the rest of the men to get horses. But none took the straw horse and when all had new horses he rode up to it.

It did not run from him.

He slid from Magpie's brown pony, patted it on the neck—it had run well for days without faltering—and slipped the end of the bridle rope from its jaw and onto the jaw of the straw-colored horse.

It stood for it and kept standing while he tied the blanket on its back and moved his water bottle and bow case. The brown pony moved in with the rest of the herd and he grabbed the long mane of the straw-colored horse and threw his leg over its back and settled onto him.

The horse acted as if they had always been together. He answered knee pressure, wheeled around, back and forth—Coyote Runs smiled, then laughed.

"You have a horse," Magpie said, riding up alongside him on a black mare with a white blaze on its forehead.

"Truly," he answered. "I hope I can keep him."

"Do not worry. You will get him. You have

done well on the raid and Sancta will give you the horse. I know it."

Coyote Runs hoped he was right but said nothing. It would not be proper.

They started north again, but now that they were around the immediate area of Fort Bliss and the bluebellies Sancta cut the herd back toward the west a bit and headed northwest, not back toward the village but off to the west of it. Riding this way they would not come back to the top of the canyons at all but out in the desert in front of them.

Coyote Runs moved over to Magpie and rode next to him for a time.

"Why is it that we do not head back for the village?" he asked.

Magpie snorted through the cloth over his mouth and nose. "You have much to learn still. You never come home directly from a raid, never show where the village is. Sancta leads us this way in case anybody follows us. We do not want to lead them back to the women and children, do we?"

It made sense and Coyote Runs wished he had kept his mouth shut. He moved the straw-colored horse back to the side and thought how stupid he was—a true warrior would have known, would not have asked, and he vowed never to ask anything stupid again.

Dust.

It grew thicker as they rode in the dark until

Coyote Runs had no idea of where he was, where he was going or where he had been. He could not see the stars, the horses in front of him—he could not even see the ears on the straw-colored horse he was riding.

All night in this manner they rode. Not fast, because it was not possible to push the large herd with any speed. If pressed, the herd would just break into smaller groups and scatter and they would lose many of them.

But they kept up a steady movement through the night—although Magpie and Coyote Runs had no idea how fast or how far they had gone—and by the time first good light came Coyote Runs was all but falling off the straw-colored horse.

Out of excitement he had slept poorly the day before and now a whole night with no rest had added to the exhaustion and brought him to the point of reeling.

He took some heart in the fact that Magpie was in no better shape. At one point he found himself riding next to his friend and saw that he had tied himself to his blanket cinch and was sound asleep, his head nodding forward on his chest.

Coyote Runs took a small cord from his bowcase and did the same thing, going around his waist and to the rope that kept his blanket in place. He was just pulling the knots tight when he heard gunfire.

In the thick clouds of dust rising in the morning air it was impossible to tell what was happening but he could hear the fire and knew whoever was shooting had large guns. The sounds were low, thudding, and the Mexican riders would not have such guns. Only the bluebellies, the pony soldiers, would make such a noise with their large rifles.

He hesitated for a moment, confused, and in that time Magpie—who had been on his left—came galloping out of the dust.

"Run! Soldiers—run, my friend, they are too many. They are amongst us. Head for the canyons. Run now!"

And he was gone, off to the right in the dust, invisible.

Still Coyote Runs held back. He was reluctant to lose the horses so easily. What would the men say if he just ran and it proved to be nothing? Besides, his medicine was strong. Had not the Mexicans shot at him and missed?

But in half a second another figure came out of the dust, then two, and he saw that they were wearing the blue wool coats of the soldiers and were holding the loud rifles and were aiming at him and he turned and dug his heels into the straw-colored horse.

It broke into a run as if waiting for the command, lunged so hard that Coyote Runs would have fallen off had he not been tied on. And the lunge saved his life, as he fell backward a soldier rode beside him and held out his rifle and fired, not ten feet away, but the bullet passed where Coyote Runs had been sitting and missed him.

Now run, he thought. Now little horse, run for all there is, run for my medicine, my life, my soul. Run like the wings of birds. Fly—runflyrunfly.

The straw-colored horse laid its ears back and streamed its tail and streaked through the sand dunes and mesquite so fast that the soldiers could not possibly have followed him, would have lost him in the thick clouds of dust.

But suddenly they broke clear into the morning sun. Running across the rear of the herd Magpie and Coyote Runs quickly moved out of the dust cloud and as they did Coyote Runs recognized where they were.

He was running straight toward the bluffs and high canyons up from the desert. Ahead of him not two hundred long paces he saw Magpie driving his horse, whipping it, and when he turned to look back he saw four soldiers break out of the dust, chasing them. Three hundred paces, no more, separated him from the four men. They all had the large rifles. One of them had been the one to shoot at him.

Four, he thought—so much noise from four men?

But there were more. Off to the side, looking to the north, he saw the main body of Apaches were being chased toward the next canyon over by more soldiers.

Firing.

Everybody was firing. The soldiers were trying to shoot while they rode. It was hard to see how they could hit anything, but Coyote Runs heard those behind him fire—the rifles making a dull thud—and then heard the whistle of the bullet passing close to him.

The canyon. How far?

Bright sun, clear morning desert air, cool morning air with the horse running so well, how far? How far to safety?

Ten, fifteen bowshots to the mouth of the canyon. And then what? If he made it, then what?

His medicine. The canyon they were heading for was the one leading to his medicine place. If he could make that, could get to the sacred place of the ancient ones, surely he would be safe. . . .

More firing, the bullets hissing past. He turned to look back once more and saw that the soldiers had fallen slightly back. They were all big men, heavy, and their mounts were not as fresh. It must have been the group of soldiers they saw on the way down—out on patrol. They must have run into them. He saw sweat on the sides of their horses, foam from their mouths. His own horse was the same, wet, but still driving well, its shoulders pumping with great strength.

O spirit, what have you given me here, he thought. What a horse.

Four bowshots left to the canyon mouth.

There he would have to leave the horse and run

up the sides on foot. If he got into the rocks they would never catch him. Not the big sweaty men in the heavy blue clothes—he would be free.

Again they fired. Again the small whistles, the little chu-chu-chu of death.

Ahead of him Magpie suddenly jerked erect on his horse and a red spray went out from his chest. He threw up his arms almost as if he were waving both hands. He began to fall forward, then fell back and to the side and was dragged by the rope around his waist. His horse tried to keep running without stepping on him but could not and veered off into a circle fighting away from the body.

The body.

Magpie.

Magpie was a body.

He must untie the rope holding him to the straw-colored horse. He fumbled with the knot, jerked, finally pulled it free. Only twenty good leaps to the canyon mouth, to the trail, to safety, to life.

Magpie was a body.

He slammed his heels into the horse, asking for more, still more speed. Behind him there was more gunfire. The bluebellies reloaded as they rode, shot again and again and still the bullets missed.

Ten leaps.

Now five.

Coyote Runs felt a slap on his leg and the horse

grunted beneath him and began to go down. They had hit the straw-colored horse. But when he looked down to the side he saw his foot hanging loosely, blood coming from just above the ankle.

They had hit him and the bullet had gone on into the horse. His medicine had failed—how could that be? He was so sure of it. . . .

No thinking now, too late for anything.

The horse collapsed, its legs getting softer and softer as it caved in and just as it hit the ground Coyote Runs fell off to the right and rolled on his shoulder. His bow, all his arrows were gone. He had no way to fight but it didn't matter now.

He was in the canyon.

The mouth of the canyon.

His medicine place—he had to reach it. It was all he could think of now, pulling himself along, and he scrabbled on his one good leg and his hands up a narrow trail, kept going though the pain came now in waves, covered him in red waves, kept pulling and fighting until he was in a grassy area.

They would not come, he thought. The soldiers would not come after him up in the canyon. He would keep going but they would not come for him. They would turn away.

He was wrong.

He heard them yelling in back of him, yelling to each other as they started up the trail after him. Their voices echoed from the canyon walls. They did not sound like men, the voices, but like devil voices, death voices, ghost voices.

He shook his head. The craziness from the wound was coming into his head and he shook it to clear it, to stop the weakness.

He needed everything now. Had to have everything in him to get away.

He fought forward on his good leg and hands, crawling and hobbling across the grassy area, the dry grass crumbling beneath him, the morning sun warm on his back.

Everything bright, everything very clear and bright and hot and fresh. The air smelled good, even through the pain; smelled sweet and good.

I will do this thing, he thought, his head momentarily clear. I will get away from the bluebellies and to the place of the sacred ones and back to my mother and ask the question of medicine, ask what I do not know.

The soldiers voices grew fainter.

I am doing this—I am making it away from them. O spirits, dust spirits and wind spirits and ghost spirits help me, come now to help me.

They were in the streamed of the canyon, down and to his right, between him and the place of the ancient ones. They blocked him. He would have to hide. He would have to find a place and hide from them and let them search until he could get around them and while thinking of it, while wondering where he could hide, his eyes caught the dark place beneath an overhanging boulder looking down on the spring.

All at the same time he saw the spring and the boulder and the dark place and knew what he had to do. His body, his whole being wanted to get to the water at the spring. He had never been so thirsty. But that was where the soldiers would look. They would seek him there.

Instead he must hide beneath the boulder. Cover himself with dirt and hide there and let the spirits take the soldiers the wrong way.

He worked in beneath the boulder, back in the crack where it met the earth, and carefully covered himself with sand and dust so that he would not show and thought still that he would do this, could do this thing.

And now they came.

Three of them. They must have left one to stay with the horses. Three of the soldiers came and he smelled them before he saw them. They smelled of strange sweat and some smell that came from the wool in their clothing and tobacco and hair on their faces— some mixed small of all that together.

White smell.

Bluebelly smell.

Pony soldier smell.

Death smell.

Then he saw them. All three were walking side by side, about ten yards apart, staring intently at the spring, the small cottonwoods, the big rifles held in front of them, ready.

Ready for him. Ready to shoot him.

Now, he thought—now must my medicine be strong and the spirits come to help me. Now there must be help.

They were so close now, so close he could see that one of them had a small cut on his cheek and that the blood had dried black. The man was large, squinting in the sun, and in the same sun, in the new morning light Coyote Runs saw his end, his death.

As he watched the soldiers begin to pass, his eyes fell on the ground in front of them and there it was, his betrayal.

His ankle had left a small trail of blood, smears here and there on the rocks and in the dirt. He had not thought of that. Had not considered that he would leave blood.

Still he had a moment of hope. They were almost past it, past the small blood trail and he thought, oh, yes, I will live yet, I will not die in this place. I will live, I will live, I will live. . . .

Then the bluebelly saw it.

The soldier on the right stopped suddenly and

looked down and Coyote Runs thought, no, not now, hide me medicine but knew, knew it was too late.

The soldier's eyes followed the scuffs and patches of blood up and to the right, up and up the eye came until he was looking at the rock.

He said something, a low word to the other two men, and they stopped.

Take me now, spirit, Coyote Runs thought— take me up and away now, away and away from this place. Take me.

They saw him.

But they did not shoot.

They walked up to where he lay beneath the overhang of the rock, stood there, strong and tall and ugly and blue and stinking of white sweat they stood there and looked down on him.

Coyote Runs did not move, lay looking up at them, sought his spirit, sought his soul. Away now, take me away from this place, spirit. . . .

The man who had first seen him said something again, not to Coyote Runs but the other two men, and they all laughed. Words Coyote Runs did not understand, but the laughter he knew. It was hard laughter.

Then the soldier said something to him.

It was some kind of order, but he could not understand it. Some strong word. Maybe he swore.

Coyote Runs looked at him, shook his head. I do not know what you mean.

Then the soldier leaned down, still smiling, and put the muzzle of his rifle against Coyote Runs' forehead and he thought, no, not now, I will go with you, I am in the wrong place, take me, spirit, take me now quickly before, before, before. . . .

There was an enormous white flash, a splattering flash of white and the start of some mad noise to end all noises and then there was nothing.

Nothingness.

10

Brennan snapped awake and sat up.

He was scared, no, worse, terrified. Short breaths, pants that puffed in and out, his eyes wide, nostrils flared and the night, the night all around and closing on him and he did not know why.

Did he dream?

He could not think wholly of it, if there had been one. There were the edges of something, some greater horror that he did not understand. A stink he did not know, and pain, horrible pain in his leg and head and it had slammed him awake.

Hard awake.

He fought to control his breathing, got it down, stared around in the darkness. There was only starlight but it made the canyon seem painted with a silver ghost brush. He could see things, boulders, canyon walls, but not in detail. As if painted and left blurry.

Take me, spirit . . .

The thought came and left before he knew he'd really had it. Just the words. *Take me, spirit . . .* in and out.

How strange. I never think these things, he thought. What is wrong with me?

Below him the others slept quietly. The fire had long since died out and even the ashes must be cold, he thought, and the word *cold* brought the night down on, into him. He was suddenly freezing, the sweat chilling him because he was sitting.

He pulled the bag up around his shoulders and shivered. By squinting he could just make out the numbers on his digital watch.

Three in the morning.

He had never been a light sleeper. Even just after his father left when his mother sat crying Brennan would sleep hard. And he never, ever had come awake suddenly so frightened, his breathing stopped.

Or thinking strange thoughts about spirits.

He lay back and pulled the bag up over his head to hold the warmth. Even in the summer, in the desert the nights were cold.

What is the matter with me? Nightmares, cold sweats.

He tried to close his eyes and doze but could not sleep. There was great unease in him, a great churning, whirling confusion that he could not understand and he sat up again.

Something.

Something was there with him, in him, around him. He could feel it. Some other thing was there.

What are you?

It finally came, the question. He asked it in his mind, then aloud, in a soft whisper:

"What are you?"

But there was no answer, no sound but a nightbird off in the canyon moonlight. A low warble, soft, there and gone. Below, his mother must have heard the sound in her sleep and turned over in her bag but did not awaken.

He was still very cold, colder than he'd ever been. He wrapped in the sleeping bag and shivered but could not seem to get warm and when he lay back on his foam sleeping pad he realized that something was sticking up beneath his shoulder, pushing into the foam.

He tossed and turned but it still seemed to be prodding him and finally in irritation he raised up the corner of the foam pad to pull it away.

It was a round and fairly smooth rock, the curve of it sticking just out of the sand beneath the sleeping pad, but when he tried to dislodge it he found that it was buried and would not come out.

He pushed and pulled at it and after some effort it began to wiggle slightly and he at last broke it loose and put it over to the side. He scraped some sand into the hole left by the rock and lay back again but in all this effort the fear, the sweat, the chills had not left him.

Take me, spirit . . .

Again it was there, or still. Who are you? he thought. Then whispered it. "Who *are* you?"

And thought, I am cracking, completely cracking up. This is crazy.

Maybe it's where I am. Maybe there is something in the wind. . . .

There was no wind. The still canyon in the moonlight seemed almost to mock him. Everything was so peaceful, so settled and beautiful, and yet there was something that would not leave him alone.

He could not sleep and again he sat up and as he did so his hand fell on the round rock he'd dug out from beneath the sleeping pad.

He started to throw it away to the side but as he made the move the light from the moon caught it and he saw it for the first time.

"What . . . ?"

It was not a rock.

It was a human skull.

He dropped it instantly, jerked his hand away and pushed back under the rock. But there it was again, a soft nudge in his thinking, a command, no, a request, a thought to do a thing he did not understand and he picked the skull up again.

It was very old. Or he thought it was very old. And

it was not complete. There was no lower jaw and it was filled with dirt and small rocks so that he could not make out the features.

He held it up in the moonlight and turned it this way and that but there wasn't enough light to see very well. He shook it to knock some of the dirt out of it and there was a small rattling and all the dirt, dried old sand, fell away.

Suddenly there were eye sockets and a hole where the nose had been and teeth, upper teeth, but the whole back of the skull was missing. There was a gaping hole where the rear curve had been and when Brennan turned it over he saw that there was a round hole in the front of the skull, just above the eyes, roughly the size of his index finger.

A bullet hole.

It was the first thing that came to mind and he should drop it, he knew, should put it down. Whoever had been the skull, whoever it was had died a violent death, a murder victim, and he was playing with evidence and yet he could not.

Could not put it down.

Take me, spirit . . .

There it was again, while he held the skull. It did not come from the skull but from some other place, outside his thinking and yet inside his mind. Some strange part of him.

And he then knew what he had to do, knew it with all the certainty he had ever felt about anything in his life. He must take the skull.

Wrong or right it was there. A fact. A known. He must take the skull from this place.

He looked below to the fire pit and they were still all asleep, even the kids. But the sky was beginning to lighten over the back of the canyon, to the east, and they would be waking soon.

He pulled his pack close to the back and opened the top compartment. In the bottom he had a spare sweatshirt and he pulled it out now and wrapped the skull in it and put it back carefully and thought all the time, all the time, I am crazy, this is crazy, I am crazy.

But he could not stop himself.

11

Brennan shook his head and looked up just as the mower began to head into a rosebush. He jerked the wheel hard sideways and slewed around the edge, so close, the rose blooms brushed his cheek as he went by.

Nothing, no part of his life was acting normally since the camping trip and the skull.

A week had passed. They had broken camp after breakfast the next morning and walked back out to the van, the kids wild all the way, and driven home and nobody knew of the skull.

When they returned home Brennan put the skull up in his closet on a shelf reserved for models, wrapped in paper. His mother rarely came in his room and never bothered the shelf, so it would be safe.

Although safe from what, safe from whom Brennan couldn't think.

He was acting ridiculous and he knew it. One side of him told him to call the police and take the skull to them and tell where he got it. The skull might not be as old as all that, might be part of a murder investigation and he would be withholding evidence. He did not know how much of a crime that was but suspected it was a serious one and he was not a criminal. Or at least had never been one.

Before now.

Crazy.

But something in him, some other part of his thinking told him to keep the skull and he could not think of a single reason why.

To know it.

That thought crept in and had been in his mind before. Every time he thought of the skull. He was supposed to know it.

Take me, spirit had been there, in his thinking, and now, *to know it.*

Know *what?*

It was so frustrating! Here he was, hiding a skull with a bullet hole in it in his closet, hiding it even from his mother, maybe breaking the law and he had no reason for it, no excuse.

Well, see, Officer, every time I thought about calling you this little thought came into my head and it said something about a spirit and that I was to know something. . . .

He wheeled the mower around another rosebush and

looked up to see Stoney glowering at him from where he was working with the string cutter around the small flower beds.

The house belonged to a judge and Brennan kept finding himself looking at the windows thinking what if the judge was home and knew he had a criminal working in his front yard.

Possible criminal, he thought, make that a possible criminal.

The week had been almost completely insane.

He no longer slept well. At night in his room he lay with his eyes open, thinking of the canyon and the moonlight and, of course, the skull.

Always the skull.

The first night back he had taken it from the closet and examined it in better light at the small desk-table in his room after his mother was asleep.

It was so small.

That was what hit him the first time. The back half of the skull was gone but even if it had been there it was a very small skull and he thought it must have been a child's skull.

So he took a tape ruler out of the drawer and measured it, across and from front to back, as best he could and then—because there was nothing else to compare it to—he measured his own skull.

They were nearly the same.

He had to press through his hair to get the tape tight down on his own skin, and make a guess at the measurement around the missing back part of the skull but when he did there was only a slight difference in the measurements and he thought then that it must have been a boy.

A boy like him.

There was no reason to think it. He would not have a much bigger skull when he was a grown man, so why could it not be a man's skull? Or a woman's or girl's skull?

Yet he could not shake the feeling and that night, the first night back, he put the skull back in the closet, went to bed but could not sleep though he was tired from the camping trip and not sleeping well the night before.

At last his eyes had closed and he felt that he was still awake but somehow he dreamed, slipping in and out of the dream.

The dream that night made no sense. He sat cross-legged on a high ridge overlooking the desert and the canyons below, apparently near where they had camped, and watched an eagle flying. It moved in huge circles, taking the light wind, climbing and falling, and he just sat and watched it fly and didn't think or say anything, didn't do anything.

He could sometimes see the eagle very closely, see the feathers, the clear golden eye, then it would swing away and go higher and higher and finally become a small speck against the blue sky and then, in the end, nothing, and he just sat all the time on the ridge watching.

Then he had opened his eyes and was awake. When he looked out the window it was light, well past dawn, and he was surprised to see the clock on his desk at seven-thirty. Stoney was due shortly and he had jumped out of bed and gone to work without eating.

All that day, and the next, and the next he had thought of the skull. And during the nights he did not sleep but lay back and closed his eyes and had strange dreams until he opened his eyes and had to go to work.

After the eagle dream he dreamed of a snake. The snake was a rattler, coiled in a lazy *S* on a rock in the sun. Brennan was afraid of snakes, snakes and spiders, but in the dream he had no fear of the snake and sat near it on a stone and watched it. The snake moved this way and that, back and forth, but not forward, the head weaving gently, the tongue flicking out in silence. Then it swung its head around and looked directly at Brennan, into his eyes, and Brennan was still not afraid. In the dream he studied the snake and the snake seemed to nod, its head moving up and down once gently, and Brennan answered the nod and was awake and the dream made no sense.

He knew nothing of snakes. Except for one dead on the highway as they drove by he had never seen a rattlesnake, knew nothing about them. But the snake seemed to know him, seemed to be trying to say something to him, and in the same dream he danced with a group of dancers in a circle, holding arms and moving to the rhythm of a drum.

In the dream he looked down and watched his feet move in the sand, kicking up small puffs of dust, and he yelled with the rest of the dancers, yelled a word he did not understand when the dance was done.

And came awake. That night he sat up in his room for close to two hours after the dream and thought he must be going crazy.

Of course he knew it came from the skull, and thought in some way that it had to do with a guilty conscience that came of not calling the police, or telling his mother. That feeling guilty was making him have bad, or at least strange, dreams.

But when he came to the edge of it the next day, telling his mother or calling the police, when the pressure grew and bothered him that much he could not do it.

It was not that he didn't want to, not that he didn't feel like it.

He couldn't.

He simply could not make himself do it and that frightened him more than having a guilty conscience. Why could he not do it?

In the third dream there was a horse.

He was riding the horse in bright sunlight and heat. The horse had light, almost yellow hair but he thought of it as having the color of straw in the dream, a straw-colored horse, and it ran beneath him, between his legs with a power that seemed to come from thunder.

The front legs pounded up and down and he felt the back legs bunch and spring each time, driving the horse forward, the front shoulders rippling against his legs, driving, pounding.

There was great joy in the run, the wind against his face, the heat on his back, which was bare, and the horse thundering across the sand and his hair blowing out in back of him, his hair blowing like the straw-colored mane of the horse. He laughed in his throat in the dream and laughed in his bed and the sound awakened him and he came awake and sat up and was glad.

Glad. His heart felt gladness and he did not know or understand why. It faded, slipped away as he sat in the dark looking at the small light on the smoke detector thinking again, or still, that he was going crazy.

On the second to the last morning, two days before the day when he would come close to wiping out the rose-bushes at the judge's house, he sat at breakfast with his mother.

She had been drinking coffee and he had a bowl of oat bran.

She was sitting in silence, sipping the coffee, looking out the window at the morning sun coming in, lost in thought, and he coughed to get her attention.

"Is it possible for crazy people to know they're going crazy?"

She studied him for a time over her cup. The famous mother look, as he thought of it. The Mother Look. The what-are-you-up-to Mother Look.

"That," she said, "is a very strange question for dawn on a Friday morning."

He didn't answer at once, thinking. "It's not me, understand. I was just wondering, you know, if someone is crazy do they know they're crazy?"

She put her cup down. "I don't think so—but I'm no expert. You'd have to ask a psychologist to be sure. . . ."

They had dropped it, and that night he had gone to bed half afraid to sleep.

And a dream had come.

This time there was another person in the dream. A girl. He could not quite see her as she moved ahead of him, walking somewhere—he did not know from where or to where—but he wanted to know her better. Wanted badly to know her. And she was gone, walking into a mist that he could not pass through, a mist that frightened him very much.

This time when he awakened he was drenched with perspiration and his mother was sitting on the side of his bed.

"You made noise," she said, "a funny sound, like words I couldn't understand. Do you feel all right?"

"A cold," he said, though he knew it wasn't true. "Maybe I'm getting a cold. . . ."

She had stayed with him until he had closed his eyes and feigned sleep but that night he did not sleep any more.

And the final day in the week he decided that he had to do something, find out what was wrong. . . .

Find out what the skull was doing to him.

And the best way to find that was to try to find out about the skull. He had to know more about it, all he could know about it.

That's where the answer was, somewhere in the skull.

12

It was one thing to say he had to learn about the skull, and quite another thing to do it.

Aside from taking it out of the closet again and looking at it—which he did on Saturday morning, turning it over and over—there didn't seem to be a way to know anything.

On closer examination in good light the skull proved to have all good teeth, no cavities. At least in the upper teeth —he did not have the lower jaw or teeth.

"Does that mean anything?" he said aloud in his room. It was early on Saturday morning and his mother was gone—off on some trip with Bill. They were growing closer and Brennan was happy for her—although it had happened many times before. Getting this close.

"It could mean he was young. . . ."

There it was again. *He.* Why did he think the skull

was male? No, why did he *know* the skull was male? Because he knew it, was certain of it.

And without any reason.

"All right." He set the skull on his desk, the eye sockets staring up at him. In a second it bothered him and he turned it sideways. "All right—so the teeth are good and that might mean it—*he*—was young. And if he was young, then the measurements could mean he was about my age."

Of course it's all guessing, he thought, leaning back. From the side he could see the damage done by the bullet. The entry hole in the forehead was a little over a half inch in diameter, and almost perfectly round. But a piece of bone as big as the palm of his hand was missing at the back, broken out in a rough oval.

God. How must that have been, he thought. How could that be? To have an explosion and then a bullet slam through your head that way and carry away the back of your skull and all the things you are, all the things you were or are or ever will be are gone then, blown away.

He shook his head. He was squinting, feeling the pain, and he tried to think of something else but could not. Instead he thought of the film he'd seen of Vietnam, an old film showing a man shooting another man in the temple on a street. It had been a television news film. He remembered the way the shock of the bullet had made the man squint.

He stood, turned away from the skull, looked out the window, and broke it then, broke the train of thought.

A week. I've had the skull a week and a day and I'm going crazy. What have I done?

He wrapped the skull up again and put it in the closet. I'll do it now, he thought, I'll call the police. . . .

But he didn't, couldn't. Instead he found himself putting his running shoes and shorts and a T-shirt on and heading out into the cool Saturday morning air.

He set an easy lope away from the house, not meaning to head in any direction but in a block he turned left and started the long road that went up and around the side of the mountain overlooking El Paso.

There was almost no traffic yet, no distractions, and he gave himself to running, did not think but increased the pace until he was driving up the mountain road, his legs pumping.

In moments the work made him sweat and he pulled his T-shirt off, still running, and rolled it and tied it around his forehead to keep the sweat from his eyes.

Running hard now, pushing himself, deep breaths, deep and down his legs knotting and bunching and taking him up the steep road, his shoes slamming on the road, no thoughts, a blank . . .

And the word *Homesley* came in.

Perfect, he thought. Homesley.

Maybe he'll know what to do.

13

John Homesley was a biology teacher in Cardiff School. Brennan had taken biology from him the year before and an almost-friendship had developed.

Well, Brennan thought, jogging down the street that led to Homesley's house, cooling from his run—it hadn't started that way.

Brennan had nearly flunked, had trouble in school, and Homesley had stopped him in front of the school one day as he was heading home at the end of the day.

He was an enormous man, tall and very heavy, bordering on fat but in a controlled way. Like a bear. He had rounded shoulders that somehow looked massively strong, with a heavy head of dark curly hair that always seemed a little long and a neatly trimmed beard filled with gray streaks.

"Did you know," he had said to Brennan, standing in the sun and grass in front of the school, "that the beetles are the most numerous species on earth?"

"What?" Brennan had been in a hurry and was slightly annoyed at the delay.

"Beetles. They're the most numerous species of life on earth. Do you suppose that means God made the earth for beetles?"

"I beg your pardon?" Brennan was confused. He had taken biology but Homesley hadn't said four words to him. As in most of his classes Brennan had taken a desk in the back of the room and spent much of his time trying to be ignored.

And now this teacher had stopped him on the school lawn and was talking to him.

"I said, beetles are the most numerous species on earth —so do you suppose that means God made the earth just for beetles? That beetles are God's favorite thing?" He stared down at Brennan, his eyes serious, but a faint smile at the corners of his mouth.

"I don't know," Brennan said, and thought, God, I sound dumb. Maybe I *am* dumb. "I guess so."

"Aren't you curious about them?"

"Beetles?"

"Yes. Don't you want to know about something that is the most numerous thing on earth?"

"Well . . . I don't know. I guess so. Yes. I guess I am curious about beetles." The sun was on him and he had to squint to look up at Homesley.

"Good. Let's find one."

"What?"

"Help me find a beetle. There's probably one within five feet of where we're standing."

And he put a pair of reading glasses on, which made his face look round and almost clownlike, dropped to his hands and knees and started looking through the grass, moving blades of grass sideways with his fingers.

Brennan stared at him. There were other kids going past and they stopped to watch.

"Come on." Homesley looked up. "Give me a hand. It's easier with two looking."

And still Brennan hesitated. Then he thought, oh, well, maybe it will help my grade and he dropped to his knees and started looking through the grass with Homesley.

"What are you looking for?" A tall kid in the eleventh grade stopped.

"Beetles," Brennan said.

"Beetles? You mean like bugs?"

"Yes," Brennan said, without looking up, wishing he could drop into a hole in the ground.

"They're the most numerous species on earth."

"Oh."

"Mr. Homesley wanted to find one and I'm helping him."

"Oh."

The boy had walked away shaking his head and Brennan kept his eyes down into the grass.

And he saw one.

A black bug, almost an inch long, a shiny black beetle. "I found one."

"What does it look like?"

"It's black and shiny and about an inch long." Brennan put his finger down and poked the beetle. It raised its hind end. He poked it again.

"It's probably a blister beetle. Don't touch it."

But it was too late. The beetle emitted a squirt of some kind of fluid from beneath its rear end, squirted it on Brennan's finger. Instantly there was a sharp burning sensation, a quick sting.

"Ow . . ."

"Exactly. They have a defense mechanism that's pretty effective. You'll hurt there for a while and might get a blister, but you'll be all right. Did you know that some beetles have a small turret gun down there and they can aim all around their body and hit with incredible accuracy?"

Brennan shook his hand. The spot on his finger hurt like a sting. "No. I didn't."

"Oh, yes, beetles are fascinating. A person could spend his whole life just studying them. Just beetles." He sat up, looking straight into Brennan's eyes, his face serious. "I can't believe you don't want to know things."

"But . . . well, I do."

"You don't seem to want to know biology."

"That's different . . . I'm just not good at it."

"Nonsense. You found the beetle, didn't you?"

"But that's not the same. . . ."

"But it is. Exactly. That's what studying biology—or anything else for that matter—is all about. Just finding things. Do me a favor, will you?"

By now there was a circle of kids watching and Brennan had never been so embarrassed in his life. He had spent most of his childhood being very shy and trying to not be noticed. And now Homesley had put him right in the middle of things.

"Every day bring me a different kind of beetle."

"What?"

"Bring me a new beetle each day and we'll learn about them together. . . ."

And a sort of friendship had developed. Brennan had done as Homesley had asked and brought a beetle, a different kind of beetle, each day and they would look it up, study the characteristics, talk about them.

And Brennan passed biology—Homesley had been as good as his word. But a strange thing had happened. Somehow working with Homesley had bled over into other parts of school. It wasn't that he enjoyed school—he wouldn't go that far.

But he studied. His habits changed and he studied almost by instinct; almost naturally.

Which just as naturally brought his grades up.

Which made his mother happy.

Which made him happy.

Which made it still easier to live, to study, to learn—all because of Homesley and his beetles.

But perhaps more important, Homesley had shown him other things as well—other than biology.

He had invited Brennan to his home one weekend, where he lived with a wife named Tricia who was almost as small as he was large.

He had taken Brennan into the basement, where Brennan had expected to find jars of bugs, or plants, or fetal pigs floating in preservatives.

Instead it looked like the interior of a space vehicle. Every corner, every wall was filled with electronic equipment.

"What . . ." Brennan stopped just inside the room.

"Music."

"Music?"

Homesley had nodded. "Trish and I love to listen to music. We can't watch television—it's too . . . slow for us —so we listen to music."

"You mean like rock?" Somehow he couldn't feature Homesley listening to wild music.

And Homesley had shaken his head.

"Mostly classical. I like Mahler, and Bach and Beethoven. Trish gets into opera."

There was an overstuffed couch in the middle of the room and at each end a floor lamp stood.

"You mean you just come down here and sit and listen to music?" he asked.

Homesley had nodded. "Sometimes we read—but usually we just listen."

"And all of this is just for music?"

Another nod. "Of course a lot of it is speakers. Would you like to try it?"

"I sure would. . . ."

"Sit on the couch, in the middle, and lean back. I'll play Mahler's Resurrection Symphony for you."

Brennan thought of asking for some Pink Floyd or Creedence Clearwater but decided Homesley probably didn't have them.

He sat.

And listened.

And it was more than just hearing the music. At first the strains of Mahler sounded soft to him, and he thought he would be bored—which was what usually happened when he listened to classical music.

But the system, the speakers made the sound so . . . so pure somehow, so rich and pure that the music went past just hearing, past listening—the music went into him.

He sat in stunned silence while the whole of Mahler's Resurrection Symphony, the whole of Mahler's music, the whole of Mahler's thinking went into his mind.

It was incredible.

When the music was finished he looked around the room expecting something, the whole world, to have changed. Homesley had left as the symphony began and he came in holding a can of soda.

"Like it?"

Brennan felt like whispering. "I didn't know, you know, didn't have any idea music could be that way. . . ."

And so Brennan learned about beetles and about music that year. Through the spring he went several times to the Homesleys' house and listened to music, talked about music, about biology, about nothing and everything and learned most about himself.

When summer arrived he went to work for Stoney and had not spent much time with Homesley. He had been working too hard.

But the friendship was still there and the feeling that Homesley was perhaps the only person who could help him with this skull business.

That's how he thought of it now.

This skull business.

No sleep, dreams he couldn't begin to understand, thoughts, voices through his brain that made no sense, his whole life upside down . . .

This skull business.

He jogged now to cool a bit coming off the run as he neared Homesley's house.

Homesley could help.

He hoped.

14

"A skull."

Homesley's voice was flat. He stared at Brennan.

Brennan nodded.

"With a bullet hole in it."

Another nod. "In the forehead."

"And you have it in your closet."

"Yes." Brennan sighed. "It seems pretty stupid, doesn't it?"

"Well." Homesley had been trimming a small green plant and he plucked a leaf from it, thinking. "Well, I don't know. Let me get all this straight. You found the skull in a canyon and brought it home without telling anybody?"

"Right."

"And you still have not called the police?"

"I can't."

"Brennan . . ."

"I mean it. I can't. I've started to several times, many times, but something stops me and I can't. I just can't. And I'm having all these weird dreams that I don't understand and things are happening to me. . . ."

He told Homesley all of it, from the camping trip to the dreams, and when he was finished Homesley leaned back and put his hands on the table that held the plants.

"My," he said. "My, my, my . . ."

Brennan felt drained, tired. "And so I thought I would come to you."

Homesley looked out the window, thinking. A fighter from Biggs Air Force Base roared over the house making a low-level run into the desert. Homesley's house was in a development not far from the runway and the fighters were frequent visitors. Strangely he didn't seem to mind the noise—although it was also true that it couldn't be heard in the soundproofed basement music room.

"I haven't seen the skull, of course," he said, thinking out loud. "So I can't say much about it. But from what you say it looks old."

Brennan nodded. "Very old."

Homesley smiled. "Well, not *very* old. Not prehistoric or even much over a hundred years old. It had to be after guns were here—there is, after all, the bullet hole, isn't there?"

Again Brennan nodded. "Yes. I'm sure that's what it is. It's neat and round in the front. . . ."

"And a large chunk carried away in the back."

"How did you know?"

Homesley smiled, a small sad smile. "I was a medic in Vietnam. I know something of bullet wounds."

"Oh."

"So—there wasn't any hair or tissue on the skull or around it, right?"

"Right. It was . . . clean."

"That means, I think, that we can assume the skull wasn't part of a recent murder and may not constitute evidence."

"You sound like a lawyer," Brennan said.

Homesley looked at Brennan, his eyes serious. "It may very well come to that—lawyers. If the skull *does* constitute evidence—you realize that, don't you?"

Brennan tried not to think of it but he had realized it.

"And that doesn't change your mind about contacting the authorities?"

Brennan hesitated. "It's not . . . my . . . mind. Sometimes I don't want to keep the skull but a thing takes over my thinking and I can't do it. Can't contact the police."

Homesley nodded. "I see. Or maybe I don't. But I think I know what you mean." He pushed the plant away and stood, walked back and forth in the kitchen, thinking and talking as he moved. Brennan almost smiled. Homesley looked exactly as he did when he was teaching—striding excitedly left and right in front of the class.

"Facts are almost nonexistent," he said, "so it's really difficult to come at this with logic."

Brennan nodded, but said nothing.

"So we take a few shots at probabilities here. Not very scientific but I think helpful. Jump in or correct me as we go, all right?"

Brennan nodded again.

"The skull was found in the canyons up by Orogrande." He named the small settlement on the highway —little more than a gas station—north of El Paso.

"Near Dog Canyon," Brennan added.

"So, Dog Canyon, if memory serves, is one of the last places where the Apaches and the soldiers fought."

"Bill said there were several battles there," Brennan said.

"Which means we can logically assume that there were probably fights in some of the other canyons—say where you found the skull."

"And that it's an Indian skull . . ." Brennan cut in.

Homesley held up his hand. "Not necessarily. We can guess that, surmise that, assume that, speculate that, but we cannot *know* that—not without examining the skull. Correction, without having an expert examine the skull. I'm not an expert at pathology but . . ."

"I thought you knew about these things," Brennan said. "I mean it's almost like a fossil, isn't it?"

"But," Homesley interrupted, and finished, "I do *know* an expert pathologist. No, Brennan, I do not know about these things." He smiled. "There are some things even I don't know. . . ."

Brennan frowned. "I'm a little worried about show-ing the skull to anybody else. Oh, God." He shrugged. "Lis-ten to me. I sound like I've got something to hide. This is crazy—just crazy."

Homesley waited a moment, then sat back down at the table. "I know this is all troubling you, but if you're going to learn anything you're going to have to get help."

"I am. You."

"I'm not enough. But if it's any help this pathologist and I are good friends and I think I can promise you he won't tell anybody about the skull."

Brennan leaned back, waiting, and realized with a shock that he was waiting for a voice in his mind to tell him what to do. Little voices in my mind, he thought—oh good, I'm waiting for little voices in my mind. Oh great.

None came.

"All right," he said, standing. "I'll go get the skull and meet you at this man's place. . . ."

"Better yet," Homesley said, rising. "I'll call him and we'll take the car and drive down there. It might make it a little easier for you if I'm with you."

"What do you mean, easier. Where does he work?"

Homesley stopped with his hand on the door. "Where a lot of pathologists work—at the morgue." And he moved out the door.

Brennan hesitated only for a moment—thought, oh, the morgue, of course—and followed.

15

The morgue.

There was a room with metal tables and bright overhead lights and Brennan did not want to be in the room.

Everything in flat white, with large sinks along the wall and drains all over the place and the constant sound of running water and Brennan followed Homesley into the room and *really* did not want to be there.

On one table was the body of an old man. He was nude, lying flat on his back with his eyes open staring at the ceiling, his body all sunken and old and very, *very* dead.

Homesley's friend—who turned out to be named Tibbets—was tall and thin, wearing a smock spattered with blood and rubber gloves. He was leaning over the body holding a scalpel about to make a cut in the top of the dead man's stomach and Brennan almost lost his lunch.

He did not, *could* not turn away—but couldn't stand it either and he stopped.

Dead.

Tibbets looked up, saw them, and stood away from the corpse and Brennan thought, thank you, thank you, thank you . . .

"The boy with the skull," Tibbets said. "The big mystery." He and Homesley exchanged looks, then Tibbets came forward and took the tennis shoe box Brennan was carrying the skull in.

"Let's see . . ."

He took the box to a side table so that Brennan—gratefully—had to turn his back on the body.

Carefully, almost tenderly, Tibbets removed the skull. Brennan had wrapped it in a towel and Tibbets removed the towel gingerly. He put the skull on the table on a small foam pad and pulled down a large magnifying glass and light.

In the harsh white light against the metal table the skull looked very small and somehow sad, forlorn.

Tibbets must have felt it as well because he seemed to take extra care.

He first gave the skull a close visual examination through the magnifying lamp, turning it this way and that, over and around, humming songs from the sixties.

Brennan stood there and watched him and tried not to think of the body on the table in back of him.

Tibbets then took a hand-held magnifying glass and

examined the skull again still closer and much more slowly. He spent a long time looking at the bullet hole and brought another small, high-intensity lamp into play, held it almost in the hole.

He nodded, broke the humming for a second, then started again.

He turned the skull over and studied the teeth one at a time.

All of this took close to ten minutes and Brennan fidgeted from foot to foot.

Finally Tibbets took out two sets of calipers and made measurements. He measured overall the size—drawing a sketch of the skull on a pad with the part that had been blown away in dotted lines—and marking the measurements in small, precise numbers.

Then he measured the eye sockets with an inner set of calipers, again writing the numbers on the sketch, and when this was done he put the instruments down and turned to Brennan and Homesley.

"Well?" Homesley asked.

"Well, I don't think the skull is evidence, so you don't have to worry. But he did die violently."

"He?" Homesley rubbed his neck, stiff from looking over Tibbets's shoulder.

"Definitely. I'll tell you first what I know for certain, then the guesses, all right?"

Brennan and Homesley nodded.

Tibbets put the skull in the center of the foam pad and brought the light close down upon it.

"First—the wound. It's definitely a bullet wound. Judging by the size of it and the damage done to the back of the skull I would say it was a very large bore rifle. Say forty-five caliber or bigger."

He paused, thinking. "The wound was done from very close range. Probably inches—less than a foot."

"How can you tell?" Homesley asked.

"Because burned powder from the charge was actually driven into the bone of the skull. The scars are still there, the marks, and for that to happen the muzzle of the weapon has to nearly be touching the victim."

Victim, Brennan thought. Victim. He felt suddenly sick, weak. Imagine how it must have been, he thought. To have somebody hold the barrel of a gun to your head and pull the trigger. "Suicide," he whispered.

"What?" Tibbets asked. Brennan's voice was so quiet, neither of the men understood it.

"Could it have been suicide?" Brennan asked.

"Almost certainly not." Tibbets pointed to the hole in the skull and the damage done to the rear. "It was such a straight-line shot it just about couldn't have been self-inflicted—the angles are wrong."

"So this man was killed by a large rifle," Homesley put in. "Shot from very close range. . . ."

"Not a man," Tibbets said.

"But you said 'he.'"

Tibbets nodded. "I did. But not a man. He was a boy."

"A boy?"

Again Tibbets nodded. "It was an Indian boy—you can tell by the skull shape—about fourteen years old."

Take me, spirit. Take me up. It rolled into Brennan's mind and he reeled with it, almost fell over.

Homesley put out a hand to catch him. "Are you all right?"

"Don't know. Air. Need air."

Tibbets shook his head. "I forget sometimes where I work and how it gets other people. Let's go out to the lounge. . . ."

But, Brennan thought, weaving as they led him out of the room—but.

But no. I am not sick.

I am not sick.

I am not . . .

Me.

I am not me.

16

"Here, have some coffee." Tibbets held out a plastic cup.

Brennan shook his head. Slow, wobbly shakes that seemed to take forever. In the lounge, on the cheap couch, he thought—I'm here. "I don't drink coffee."

"Drink this anyway," Tibbets said. "It will take the shock away."

"A Murphy drip," Homesley said, looking at Tibbets, who nodded.

Brennan took a sip. It tasted like oil drained from a car. Sludge. "What's a Murphy drip?"

Homesley smiled that sad smile again. "We were both medics in Nam—that's where we met. A Murphy drip is something medics use. . . ."

"But what is it?"

Tibbets cut in. "You boil coffee down to a thick black solution. It's solid caffeine. When a man gets hit sometimes the shock—wound shock—will kill him even if the wound doesn't. You need a fast, raw stimulant and when we didn't have one we'd use the coffee."

"But what if they couldn't swallow?" Brennan was having trouble swallowing himself.

"No—you don't understand. We gave it anally. That was the only way to get it into the system fast enough to do any good. . . ."

Brennan looked at Homesley, who nodded to him. "That's right."

"But that's . . . that's awful."

"All of it—all of Nam was awful."

Tibbets looked over Brennan at something nobody else could see and nodded. "All of it . . ."

Homesley coughed. A soft sound. "Well—back to the present. Or the past. Finish telling us about the skull."

Brennan sat forward. Whether from the coffee or just getting out of the examining room he felt more alert.

"As I said—it was a boy of about fourteen. The teeth show little wear. Death was instantaneous and probably happened between 1860 and 1890—I would lean toward 1865 or so."

"You can tell all that from the skull?" Brennan was amazed.

Tibbets shook his head. "No. There is other knowledge involved, and I'm guessing a bit now." He thought for a moment. "It's a good bet that he was killed by soldiers—they used large-bore rifles and killed Indians. And the center of Indian—Apache—action in the canyon area was about 1860. It's just a guess. . . ."

He looked at Brennan. "You didn't say specifically where you found the skull—just in the canyons up by Alamogordo. Is it secret?"

Brennan shook his head. "Not from you. It was near Dog Canyon, a canyon south of it or maybe two. I don't know the name of it."

"All of those canyons are on National Forest land," Homesley said. "It probably goes without saying but you're not supposed to take things away."

Brennan didn't say anything, just looked at him.

"Well. In case you didn't know it . . ."

"I have to get back to work." Tibbets stood. "I have a suggestion—if you want some help."

Brennan nodded. "I sure do."

"You still know almost nothing about the skull—or rather about the boy who was the skull. You need more information."

"Where do I get it?"

"You could ask the Apaches up at White Mountain Reservation above Alamogordo. They might be able to help."

"I can't get up there," Brennan said. "I have to work. . . ."

"Or you can contact the other side—the army."

Homesley stood up. "Better yet—I have a friend who works in Denver in the Western Historical Archives. We'll write to him and ask him for any information he might be able to get us."

Tibbets stopped with his hand on the knob to the examining room door. "Ask him for all military reports, especially after-action reports for the time between 1855 and 1885." He nodded to them and went back to the body on the table before Brennan could thank him.

Homesley pointed to the exit. "Should we go do the letters?"

Brennan followed him out but stopped in the parking lot near the car. He held the box with the skull in front of him. Not like a skull, a bone fragment, but as a person. He felt a sense of urgency that he could not understand any more than he understood anything else that was happening to him.

Homesley looked at him over the top of the car. The sun was baking the metal and heat waves rose, made his face seem to move. "What's the matter?"

Brennan hesitated. "Well, I don't want to seem ungrateful but . . ."

"But what?"

"Do you think that if I paid for it we could call your friend in Denver? It will take days and days to send and wait for letters. . . ."

Homesley shrugged. "Sure. Why not? Let's go. . . ."

And Brennan had one fleeting thought as he got in the car.

Why didn't my mother meet this man and have me and he would be my father and . . .

He shook his head and sat back in the hot seat as they drove across El Paso.

17

It was easily the longest week in his life.

He worked hard with Stoney all week and called Homesley every night and when he learned nothing he ran, ran each night until he was tired and fell into bed and slept hammered into the pillow. There were no dreams.

"It takes some time to find all the stuff we asked for," Homesley said the first time he called. "Be patient."

It was easy to say, but very hard to do.

The skull was in his closet, in the box.

Waiting.

He couldn't shake the feeling that it waited—sat in the box and waited for . . . for . . .

He didn't know.

But the pressure was there, tremendous pressure, and just when it seemed he would explode Homesley called.

"It's here."

"I'll be right over."

"It's nine o'clock in the evening and there are several boxes. . . ."

"I don't care. I'll tell Mom I'm staying over—if it's all right, I mean."

"Of course it is." Homesley didn't hesitate. "We'll put you on the couch in the music room."

Brennan cleared it with his mother and was gone out the door, almost before she nodded.

He tried not to run fast the three miles or so to Homesley's—tried to set an easy pace. But he couldn't hold it. His legs, his mind, the skull took over and soon he was running at a dead lope and when he arrived at Homesley's he was sucking wind, his chest heaving.

"You must have run hard all the way," Homesley said, watching him try to catch his breath. "Are you all right?"

Brennan nodded. "Where is the stuff from the archives?" he gasped.

"In the music room."

There were seven boxes, each about a cubic foot in size.

Brennan picked up one of the boxes, put it down, picked up another. He didn't know where to start. He picked up another one and tore the top open.

Inside were photocopies of papers. Hundreds of sheets laid sideways in manila folders.

He pushed back the corner of one folder.

"Eighteen eighty-one," he said aloud. "He's dated each one. The work—the work he's done. It's incredible."

"Like I said." Homesley sighed. "He's a friend."

"He must be a very *good* friend."

"The best."

"Vietnam?"

Homesley nodded silently. "Were you all friends that way?"

Another nod. "Those of us who made it." He turned away and picked up another box. "He has them in order—see? There's a number on the side of each box. Also, there's a letter."

He opened a manila envelope and read aloud. "The boxes are in order by date. They start in 1855 and end in 1895. Inside each box the papers are also by date. There are army reports and letters and newspaper clippings. He goes on about some private stuff here, then he says he isn't sure what we want but he thinks there might be something for us in the box marked number three."

Brennan picked up the number three box and sat on the couch, opened it.

"Eighteen sixty-four," he read from the first folder.

He pulled out some papers that proved to be copies of old newspapers. Even as copies it was easy to tell that the original paper had been old. The newsprint was uneven and the headlines almost screamed.

" 'More raids by Apaches,' " Brennan read aloud.

" 'Livestock stolen, settlers frightened, army increases patrols.' "

"Got into their headlines, didn't they?" Homesley said. "They didn't need to write the story after that."

Brennan read the story. It said that there had been several raids in the area south and west of El Paso. That ". . . great damage has been caused." He finished the article. "It's so weird to read this—it's like it just happened. Yesterday or something."

Homesley set the boxes on the coffee table in front of the couch. "It's going to take days to go through all this—and we really don't even know what we're looking for, do we?"

Brennan shook his head. "Not really. But I'll know when I find it—I think."

He sat back on the couch with the box in his lap and started with the first folder. In moments he was lost in the papers.

He did not see Homesley leave, did not see Homesley come back with a plate of chocolate chip cookies and glass of milk, did not see Homesley put them on the table next to the boxes, did not see Homesley leave.

Brennan knew nothing but the papers, the papers and the world they showed.

Dust and heat. The newspapers spoke of patrols and raids and heat and dust. Long patrols the army made when the soldiers had to cut the veins on their horses and drink the blood; dust and sand so thick, they had to cover their mouths with bandannas just to breathe.

Brennan read the newspaper articles and stories first. They were all poorly written, redundant—they would often say the same thing several times.

"Twenty soldiers attacked a marauding band of Apaches in a running battle," a story said. "No soldiers were injured though several Apaches were seen to have been hit." And later in the same story: "A roaming patrol of twenty soldiers attacked a band of wild Apaches. After a brisk exchange of fire several Indians were hit though no soldiers received wounds."

He put the article aside without looking up, without seeing the cookies or milk, took another story.

This one spoke of the ranchers who had to take their families into El Paso because they feared an Indian attack.

Ranchers, Brennan thought—how could they ranch? The area around El Paso was hot, dead desert; sand dunes and mesquite and a few coyotes. How many ranchers could there be?

Again, nobody was hurt.

There was much writing of fear:

Indian Fright!

Ranchers Flee!

Citizens Terrorized!

But when he got into the articles he found that while livestock had been driven off, there had been no injuries caused.

Or very rarely.

Some prospectors had been attacked at their mine and one had died of wounds received in the battle—while four Indians were killed in the same fight.

So violent, Brennan thought, leaning back. He saw the cookies and milk and took some. Everything was so violent—white, red, color didn't seem to matter. Violence was the way of it—the engine that seemed to drive the West was violence.

All the articles were about Indian uprisings but on one copy, part of another article had been copied as well. It told of two soldiers who had hacked each other to death with knives in a cantina in Juárez. The author didn't seem shocked so much as amazed that they would kill each other at the same time.

Brennan finished the cookies and drank some milk.

Then he started to read again.

He read some of the articles in the box and opened the other boxes and scanned the articles in those as well.

But he could not forget the comment about box number three and how it might have something for him. They had told Homesley's friend—he was named Ted Rainger—only that they desired information about the canyon area north of Fort Bliss and any actions that took place there between 1860 and 1890 or so.

The third box concerned El Paso and Fort Bliss and the canyons but it took some time to go through the other boxes to make sure.

He looked up one more time, saw that the wall clock said one in the morning, and knew he should try to sleep.

But he could not stop reading. He started into the general papers in the third box. They were mostly action reports with a fair number of letters.

The action reports were paperclipped to the order to which they applied.

"You will take your patrol to the vicinity of Hueco Flats where you will sweep north and south of the road from Carlsbad, engaging any hostiles encountered unless the enemy force is too large for engagement to be prudent. You will carry twenty rounds of ammunition per man and such rations for man and horse as deemed suitable for an eight-day patrol. [Signed] Captain John Bemis."

And clipped to the patrol order was the report of the patrol leader.

"We patrolled as per instructions the area of Hueco Flats with a fifteen-man unit all in standing good health, man and horses, and the patrol was without incident until noon of the fourth day when the patrol came under fire from small arms. No men were hit though one mount sustained a mortal wound. Fire was returned and a group of approximately twelve hostiles was seen to leave an arroyo a hundred yards distant and ride south at a good pace. No hits were registered and no pursuit was given. The rest of the patrol was without event, arriving back at Fort Bliss on 12 September 1864."

Brennan put down the folder holding the orders and visualized what he had just read.

The words were so dry, concise, but they meant so much. Horses running, men shooting at other men—men trying to kill other men. A horse hit going down, everybody yelling, the Indians riding out of the arroyo and the soldiers firing at them.

What was that like? To aim at another person with a gun to try to kill him. How could that be?

He saw the clock again.

Two in the morning now. I have to work tomorrow, he thought—no, today. I have to work today with Stoney. I should lie down and sleep. Right now. I should lie back and sleep and rest, but he could not.

Instead his hands took another folder out of the box and he began to read. And then another, and another, and he read until it was past four, until his eyes burned and his brain was so full of words, of reports and more reports, that he fairly reeled with them, read until he was on the edge of something like sleep. . . .

And then he found it.

19

It started with a patrol order much like the others.

"You will patrol the area north of Fort Bliss along the line of bluffs leading to Alamogordo, over to the base of the Organ Mountains and back to the originating point. The purpose of said patrol to maintain the public order and engage hostiles if engagement seems prudent."

Brennan's mind perked. The "bluffs leading to Alamogordo" was the canyon area. This was the first patrol order in that area. But it was the after-action report that held him.

"Reporting on patrol 21 Oct. 1864. We worked due north of Fort Bliss without incident. On the second night, approximately thirty miles north of the originating point, our pickets reported hearing horses in the night but no contact was made with the suspected hostiles.

"We rode north two more days with no contact.

While making the sweep across to the Organ Mountains the patrol intersected a group of hostiles driving a herd of approximately 100 horses.

"Chase was given with the troop in skirmish formation. The main body of hostiles abandoned the horse herd and escaped in the direction of White Sands.

"Two hostiles bringing up the drag on the herd were seen to break away and ride toward the canyons in the line of bluffs to the east.

"Four troopers—O'Bannion, Rourke, Daneley, and Doolan—were dispatched and gave chase. One of the hostiles was killed in a running fight and the second was cornered in a canyon south of Dog Canyon. The troopers reported that after a brisk exchange of fire the second hostile was killed. Due to the remaining length of the patrol the bodies were not returned."

"Chaaach!" Brennan's breath exploded. He had been holding it without realizing it. A canyon south of Dog Canyon.

A coldness was in him now, a deep feeling of certainty. There was no real reason for it, for the sureness, but he was absolutely positive the skull belonged to the "hostile" the soldiers had chased into the canyon.

The canyon.

He had run then, run from them up into the canyon. One boy, his age, his own age, one boy running and four men after him.

Names. He knew the names of the men. All Irish.

Probably big men, soldiers, blue uniforms, hot, stinking of sweat, chasing him, chasing me into the canyon up beneath the rock. . . .

He shook his head, rubbed his eyes. Not me, *him*— not me. The two kept mixing in his thinking. The soldiers chased him, not me. I am sitting here reading about it—not running into the canyon away from them, trying to hide. . . .

The clock again. Five-thirty now. There were no windows in the basement but outside the sun would be up. It was morning.

He took out another packet of papers from the same folder.

Letters. The copies were all the same size but it was easy to see that they had all been written on different sizes of paper, at different times and by different people.

He riffled through them, wondering if he had time to read them. He almost put them aside but remembered Homesley's friend Rainger had worked hard to organize everything. The letters must mean something or they wouldn't be there.

He rubbed his eyes again. Two hours before he had to go to work.

He read the first letter.

20

"To the commanding officers of Fort Bliss.

"Hoping to find you in good health I take up my pen in a matter most urgent.

"Here at the Quaker school and home we meet often with both young and old Apaches. As you know we are in God's work to help these people and bring them to grace.

"These are violent times and require more open methods than in more civilized eras and so I shall come to the point.

"Thursday last I was approached by an older Indian woman from the Horse Mesa band of Apaches. I had not seen any member of that band in some time and could only hope that they were off hunting.

"But she informed me that such was not the case and her band had made a raid to steal horses in Mexico.

"On the raid two young boys were killed. One boy was named Magpie and your soldiers apparently shot him while riding and his body was recovered.

"The second boy was seen to enter a canyon with some troopers chasing him.

"This second boy was named Coyote Runs and the old woman was either his mother or his maternal grandmother. These relationships are sometimes hard to understand but I think she was the boy's mother.

"She said since they cannot find a body would I use my good offices to ask the army if they truly killed her son and if so, would they tell her (me) where the body is so she may retrieve it and give it a proper burial.

"I remain your respected servant,

"(Mrs.) Amelia Gebhart."

Coyote Runs, Brennan thought—his name, the skull's name, was, is, Coyote Runs.

"Coyote Runs." He said it aloud. A boy my age named Coyote Runs ran into the canyons with four soldiers after him. Firing at him.

I fear.

I fear for you now, Coyote Runs, I fear for you.

He put the letter down, picked up the next, which proved to be an answer.

"Dear Mrs. Gebhart.

"Having received yours of last month I take leave to reply.

"Regarding your request concerning the action of a patrol in the area of the canyons adjacent to Dog Canyon, I fear I have not much help for you.

"I have spoken personally with the officer in charge of the patrol and subsequently the four troopers who were personally involved in the aforementioned action.

"Their report assures me that while they did dispatch two hostiles in a running fight the second Indian was also killed in the running fight. Due to the heat and the remaining time of the patrol there was no attempt to recover the bodies of either man.

"It is to be expected that in the heat and with the number of coyotes this year nature may have taken its course, not to put too delicate a turn to it.

"I am sorry to have been of so little help.

"Your respectful servant,

"Col. John McIntire (Comd.)"

He's lying, Brennan thought. Whether he knows it or not, he's not telling her the truth. I found the skull up in the canyon, way at the back. With a hole in the forehead. There is no way he could have moved after being hit that way.

What was it Tibbets had said?

Oh yeah, instantaneous death.

Coyote Runs had come into the canyon. They had chased him.

He must have been hurt. Maybe his horse fell or something. Maybe they wounded him.

He had run from them but they had cornered him under the rock and shot him in the head.

Wait.

More—there was something more. There, yes, there it was—Tibbets had said the muzzle of the weapon had been held right against the boy's head.

They hadn't killed him.

They had executed him.

Run to earth like an animal, run to a hole like some frightened animal and they had found him and leaned down and put the barrel of the rifle to his forehead, put it right there and pulled the trigger.

"Oh."

Brennan blinked, put a finger to his forehead. There. There.

And Coyote Runs and all the things he would ever be ended then, in that instant.

Brennan put the papers on the table and leaned back. Tears moved slowly down his cheeks.

To know him—to know his name and how he must have died and lived.

No. That was wrong.

He knew his name now and how he died but he knew nothing of how Coyote Runs must have lived.

The door opened slowly and Homesley was standing there. He was holding a steaming cup.

"It's time to get up," he said. "I brought you some herbal tea . . ." His voice trailed off. "You've been up all night."

Brennan wiped his cheeks with the back of his hand and took the tea. He held it with both hands and smelled the strong herb steam. "Thank you."

"You found out something." Homesley said it not as a question but as a statement of fact. "Something about the skull."

Brennan sipped the tea. "His name was Coyote Runs and four soldiers executed him."

Homesley sighed. "Things never change."

"I want to know more," Brennan said. "I want to know all about him, how he lived, how it was for him to be."

Homesley nodded. "I understand."

"There is a thing I must do—I know what it is now."

Homesley said nothing, waited.

"A thing I am supposed to do."

Still Homesley waited.

"I have to take him back."

"Back where?"

"Back to where he is supposed to be."

"Where is that?"

"I'm not sure, exactly. Somewhere up in the canyons. He'll . . . tell me when it's right."

"He'll *tell* you?"

"I know how that sounds—crazy. And maybe I am. But it has to be—this has to be done."

"I understand."

And Brennan could see that he meant it. "I'll go get the skull—go get Coyote Runs. Do you suppose you could take me up to the canyons and drop me for a couple of days? I'll tell Mother I'm going camping. . . ."

"Sure. No sweat. I'll take a sleeping bag and go with you."

"We'll take our time and see the country up there. . . ."

And Brennan was only half right. He would certainly see the country—but it wouldn't be leisurely, and it wouldn't be with anybody.

21

Bill's car was parked out front and Brennan could sense something as soon as he entered the house—in the air. A tightening tension.

"Is that you, Brennan?" His mother heard the door open and close. "Come into the kitchen, please."

Her voice was flat, but not angry.

Brennan went into the kitchen.

The scene seemed frozen.

Bill sat on one side of the table and his mother sat on the other. Bill's eyes were wide, curious; his mother had some of the same look to her face mixed with concern.

Between them, on the table, sitting on a towel was the skull.

The skull.

Ahh, he thought. Ahh—there it is.

"Do you have an explanation for this—this hunk of bone?"

Yes, Mother, I do, he thought. His name is Coyote Runs and he died when an American soldier put the muzzle of a rifle to his forehead and blew his brains out. But his mouth didn't say the words. Instead his lips opened and he said, "I found it when we were camping."

"And brought it home without telling me?"

Brennan shrugged. "There were all those kids with us and I didn't want to make a mess. . . ." It sounded lame and he knew it, let it trail off.

"That was National Forest land," Bill said, his voice prim. "You're not supposed to remove things from National Forest land. . . ."

"Coyote Runs."

"What?" Bill asked.

"Not 'things,' not 'hunk of bone.' His name was Coyote Runs. He was a fourteen- or fifteen-year-old Apache boy killed by the army."

"How could you know all that?" Bill asked.

"Research. We . . . I've been doing some research." He thought it best not to mention Homesley.

"See?" His mother put her hand on Bill's arm. "I told you we didn't have to call the police."

"You were going to call the police?" Brennan asked.

"We already did," his mother said. "They should be here any minute."

"Ahh, Mom . . ."

And he could see it all then—everything. He could see the police coming in and the questions they would ask and what they would have to do—take the skull. They would have to confiscate the skull and it would go back to the National Forest, back to the government and they would put it on display in a museum somewhere, stick it in a glass case with a little plaque saying what it was and he could see it.

See it all.

And as he saw that he also knew what he had to do; what he had to do immediately.

He must take Coyote Runs back. He must follow the dreams, the instructions in the dreams. Now it was all there, all clear; he knew what would happen and knew what he must do.

He must take Coyote Runs home.

He grabbed the skull from the table, made for the back door.

"Brennan." His mother's voice stopped him. "What are you doing?"

"Mother . . ." There was nothing he could say to make it right for her; no words to explain what he had to do. "Mother—I have to leave for a few days."

"Why?" She stood. "What are you talking about?"

"He . . . needs me to do something."

Outside he heard a car pull up in the driveway. The police were arriving. Great, he thought—just great. Now I'm running from the police. I haven't done anything wrong and I'm running from the police.

"Who?" his mother asked. "*Who* needs you to do something?"

Brennan raised the skull. "Him."

"The *skull*?"

"Coyote Runs. He needs me to—well, just needs me."

"But Brennan . . ."

"I'll be back in two or three days. I have to do this. . . ."

"But . . ."

"Mother. Please."

"But . . ."

And she either nodded or he thought she nodded. Either way it no longer mattered. Time was gone.

Brennan moved through the back door and was gone.

22

The darkness seemed complete, thick, black, close around him, and he took it as a friend. There was a time when he was afraid of darkness and it surprised him faintly that he had changed.

Changed so much.

He had set an easy pace north. For all of the day, through the morning and into the afternoon he jogged lightly through the city and out past the suburbs and Fort Bliss and into the desert.

Fifty, sixty miles.

It was between fifty and sixty miles to the canyon country where he had found the skull. He remembered that from the camping trip.

He had never run or walked any distance like sixty miles—across a desert—yet he did not doubt he could do it.

The skull—Coyote Runs—would help him. He did not know how, or why, or where he was going but he knew he was not alone.

Take me, spirit . . .

Fort Bliss extended some miles north of El Paso—missile-firing and artillery-impact ranges overlapping. Signs along the road warned of unexploded artillery shells. For that reason Brennan stayed along the road until he thought he was well past the last signs, then he turned into the desert.

He had stopped at a convenience store and purchased a small knapsack and a couple of granola bars and a quart of bottled water. He put the skull and water in the pack and adjusted it to ride loosely on his back.

When darkness had first caught him he stopped and lay against the side of a sand dune to rest and stretch his legs. He had rested several times during the day just for ten or fifteen minutes each time to keep his legs from cramping. He had also drunk most of the water—amazed how fast a quart seemed to go.

He had stopped using the water in midafternoon, when the sun was hottest, and as he lay in the dark to rest he felt his cracked lips with his fingers. They were bloody. He had taken a small mouthful of water then, enough to wet his lips, and gone into a fitful kind of half sleep.

When he opened his eyes it was pitch dark, dark that wrapped him, and he thought for a moment how nice a fire would be. There was a chill in the air and dampness that came down on him.

I won't be able to see to move, he thought.

But as soon as the thought came he began to make things out. Clumps of mesquite on sand dunes, openings between the dunes appeared first as shadows, then took on solid shape and meaning.

There was enough light from the stars and a sliver of a new moon for him to see where he was going.

Off in the night he heard the faint sound of cars on the highway as they passed.

He stretched, bent at the waist and pulled at the backs of his leg muscles until they almost snapped.

Then he put the pack on his back and started off, moving easily between the dunes. He found the Big Dipper then the North Star and he set off to follow it.

And he knew things then without knowing how it was he could know them.

It was this way in the old times.

The voice—more a felt sound, an echo in his mind, than an open sound. It was his own voice, in his mind, but not his mind.

It was this way in the old times that when a man ran in the desert at night he would push a stick ahead through the sand for the small snakes.

Brennan found a length of mesquite, broke it off about four feet long. One end had a slight curve and he held this end to the ground so that it slid along the sand.

He started moving again, a half run, half shuffle, the stick sliding along in front of him.

A good trick, my friend, he thought. I had not thought of snakes. My friend. Yes. My friend.

It was this way in the old times that when a man was thirsty he would find the stalk of the plant with long quills and eat of it and find sweet water.

The plant with long quills? What could that be?

Oh. The yucca. That must be what he was talking about.

He turned out a sidewinder that had been half buried in the sand. He flicked it off to the side with the stick and it buzzed angrily before looping off to the side in the darkness.

And I knew that, he thought. I knew he wouldn't bother me.

I *knew* it.

Off to the edge of a dune he saw a yucca plant, the spiny base looking like a porcupine hunkered in the shadows. He went to the plant and squinted, trying to see better in the darkness.

Sticking straight up from the center of the plant was a stalk about three feet long. He pushed at it, touched it, and found it to feel heavy, soft.

He worked it back and forth and broke it off even with the base down in the spines.

With a little more effort he broke the stalk in two and put one broken end to his lips.

The end fairly dripped with liquid. He tasted it and found the fluid to be a sweet-tasting water—almost like watermelon.

He bit and chewed on the stalk, eating it a few inches at a time, swallowing the sweet water gratefully before spitting out the pulp and taking another bite.

Thank you.

It was this way in the old times. . . .

Thank you. He ate the whole stalk as he trotted, broke and ate another and moved through the night in the easy trot, refreshed by the sweet juice from the yucca and the coolness of the desert night.

Well before dawn he sensed light, felt the temperature drop a bit more and stopped to rest.

No. It is not time to stop.

But . . .

They are too near. We must not stop.

What . . .

Go now. Keep going now.

I am tired. I am so tired, he thought. But his legs kept driving, pushing, pounding.

Another snake—this time not a sidewinder but a larger rattler—was pushed into a warning rattle by the stick.

Brennan moved easily a step to the right as it struck at the stick and kept moving. This, he thought, from a boy who was afraid of spiders and snakes.

He had changed in some basic way. He was still Brennan but more, much more, so that he was part of the night and part of the desert and part of the sky and part of the snake and knew these things, knew all about them and did not fear them.

Into the light from dawn he moved; until the buttes and canyons rose above him to the right, he moved; until he could see boulders and lines he moved. He could not, not move.

Stop.

The thought, word, feeling, cut through the fatigue, the movement, and he stopped.

It was here. Here where the pony soldiers found us and chased us and brought Magpie down. His chest went out before him.

Here.

Brennan felt an enormous sense of sadness, a deep remorse. An old friend died here. A close friend.

And here we ran, and here, my horse running well but not fast enough and there by the cut across the land they hit my horse, hit my leg and I was down.

Brennan felt it, knew it and fell to his knees.

Here—it was here that it all happened.

He heard noises, heard sounds and thought for a moment that time had warped and that he would turn to see the soldiers riding at him.

But the sound was real.

Voices.

He heard voices out ahead—faint. Near the canyon mouth.

He held his breath and listened.

Men. It was the sound of men talking. He could not

understand the words but heard them as a low sound, a familiar low sound.

Then he heard one voice he knew.

His mother's.

His mother had come with men to look for him.

To stop him.

"Mother," he said half aloud. "Mother is here with some men."

He moved closer to the voices, keeping sand dunes and low bush between them for cover and staying low.

When he was fifty yards away he stopped again, lowered to his stomach, and—dragging the pack—made his way closer until he lay not thirty feet from his mother.

She was dressed in jeans and tennis shoes and was wearing one of Brennan's old jackets. There were two sheriff's deputies standing near her, and Bill, and off to the side a few paces, Homesley.

"He hasn't been acting normally," Brennan's mother was saying. There was worry in her voice. "Ever since the camping trip when he found the skull."

The deputies said nothing for a moment. One of them nodded to her and the other looked up into the canyons and coughed politely into his hand. "You think he ran here from El Paso in one day and a night. . . ." The tone of his voice was clearly skeptical.

"Maybe not yet." His mother stopped the deputy. "I don't think he could be here. But we have to stop him *before* he gets into the canyons. I'm worried about what may happen if he goes up in there alone."

"He'll be fine." Homesley had been silent all this while, standing off by himself. But he moved toward the others now. "There's nothing whatever wrong with Brennan. He just has something he must do."

"What?" His mother's voice was sharp, hard-edged.

"I'm not sure. Something with the skull. Maybe take it back. I don't know for certain."

"It appears to me," Bill cut in, "that if you hadn't helped him with all this, none of this would be happening."

"No." His mother held up her hand. "None of that. Brennan has learned a lot from Mr. Homesley—I won't hear people throwing blame around. There's nobody to blame about anything—I'm just worried about Brennan."

Good for you, Mother, Brennan said to himself silently. I could end it here, just stand up and end it. What am I doing anyway? This is crazy, wacko.

But his legs did not move him. He did not stand.

Instead he slid backward on his stomach until a dune with mesquite all along the top hid him. It would be a simple matter to walk around them and head up into the canyon.

But a new sound stopped him.

Engine. Truck engine. He worked forward on his elbows, dragging the pack with the skull up to the top of the dune where he lay in the mesquite and could see all below where the desert road ended in front of the canyon.

Bill's van was there, and the sheriff's car with the engine running.

But now a carryall wagon pulled up. On the side were written the words MOUNTAIN RESCUE.

It came to a halt in a swirl of sand and two men jumped out. They were dressed in climbing clothes.

"We came as fast as we could," one of them said to the deputies. "How long has he been lost?"

"Who are these people?" Brennan's mother asked.

"Rescue is always called in when somebody is lost." The deputy shrugged. "It's standard procedure. Always."

"But he's not lost," his mother said. "At least I don't think so. . . ."

"Still."

"How long has it been?" the rescue man repeated. "Dehydration may be setting in while we stand here talking."

Not likely, Brennan thought, remembering the yucca stalk. Then he felt like a snot—here all these people just cared about him, were worried about him. And he was treating them like they were enemies. Well, he thought—enough of this. He wouldn't let his mother worry.

He stood up.

23

It was like a scene from a bad movie. The boy gets lost, Brennan thought, and they find him in the nick of time and everybody lives happily. . . .

"There he is!" one of the rescue men yelled. "Right there!"

Brennan was only fifty feet away from them and looked at his mother.

"I didn't want any of this," he said. "Not for you to worry—none of it."

"I know," she said. "But . . ."

"I have to do this," he said.

Homesley stepped forward. "I brought them when your mother called me. She was worried."

"I know. It doesn't matter." Brennan stopped. The deputies and the men from the rescue unit were spreading out.

"You ran here in one day?" Homesley asked.

"And a night. Yes. He taught me what to do."

"Remarkable."

"Just a minute." Brennan held up his hand. "What are you doing?" The men had moved apart, slowly, seemingly without reason, but always apart so that they now faced him but spread away from each other.

"Nothing," one of the rescue men answered, smiling. "Why?"

"Don't come after me. . . ."

"You have to realize that you can't just take off up into the canyon."

"Why not?" Brennan tensed his legs. He closed his hand tightly on the knapsack holding the skull. They were going to come for him. My God, they were going to make a move on him.

"We have your mother's call that she was worried about your . . . status. You might be depressed, upset—we can't allow you to go up there alone. You might get into trouble. We can't allow that."

"I take back my complaint." Brennan's mother brushed hair out of her eyes. The morning sun was directly in her eyes and she had to squint. It made her look like a picture he'd seen of her when she was young, squinting into the camera, and Brennan smiled.

"It doesn't matter," the rescue man said. "He could still get hurt—he can't be allowed to go up there alone. . . ."

"Run, Brennan," his mother yelled suddenly. "Go now!"

It surprised Brennan so that for an instant he did not move. But only for an instant. The two rescue men jumped suddenly toward him and the deputies moved to the side to get between Brennan and the canyon mouth.

Brennan moved without thinking. He virtually fell backward off the dune through the mesquite and brush.

His legs windmilled beneath him and he somehow landed on his feet. The two rescue men came loping around both ends of the dune, arms outstretched to grab him.

He had one moment when he almost smiled—wondering what they were supposed to be "rescuing," then he felt their hands on his arms.

He rolled left and right quickly, slipped from their grip, and was away.

Now, he thought—or thought he thought. *Now away. Up into the canyon.* The voice was there, in him, of him, around him.

Take me, spirit . . .

He scrambled up the trail, heard the men coming behind. They were experienced at climbing, in good shape, but Brennan moved faster. His feet found the old trail and he ran lightly, exulted in his freedom. I can fly, he thought, and made the mistake of looking back.

Looking back once to see if the two men were gaining on him. His right foot came down on a rounded stone and his ankle turned. He felt/heard it pop.

An almost-click and pain roared up his leg and he went down on his side.

No.

It was this way before. They came and I was hurt in one leg. Do not stop. Do not stop. Do not stop. You must not stop. Ever.

They had him. He felt their hands grabbing him.

"No!"

One leg, he thought. I have one leg.

On his hands and the one good leg he rose, looked into, directly into the face of one of the rescue team.

"Listen," the man said. "Take it easy and listen to me. We don't want to hurt you . . ."

But Brennan didn't hear him, didn't see him, didn't see the rescue man.

His eyes were wide, he felt the heat and dust and heard his own breathing as wind whistling and echoing in some empty place.

And he saw a cavalry soldier.

Saw the blue wool of his uniform, the skin of his neck over the collar of his tunic, the stains from his sweat; smelled the horse in his clothing, saw the stubble on his chin.

All real.

"No!" he screamed again, and kicked backward with his one good leg and broke loose once more.

Then up.

Then up into the rocks and the heights of the canyon. Never to stop.

Up to safety.

Up.

24

They would not give up.

Two of them.

They must have left their horses at the bottom of the
canyon.

Good.

Even with one bad leg no bluebelly on foot could catch
him. No two bluebellies could catch him.

I am, he thought.

I am Apache!

He fought the pain down, made his mind think of
other things. His mother. *See his mother bending down to pick*
up wood. See his mother how she works. See how she builds the
fire and moves the pot onto the flame. See . . .

Brennan shook his head.

Can't, he thought. Can't remember things that never
happened to me. How can that be?

He looked back. The men had fallen still farther behind. His leg was on fire but he was moving well. Sweat poured down his face and he wiped it away with the back of his wrist.

Where?

Where am I going?

He recognized parts of the canyon from the camping trip. Even limping he was making good time.

But where?

The canyon rose above him, around him. But the canyon would come to an end. He remembered that as well.

Back up there it ended, he thought, looking to the cliffs that marked the rear of the canyon. And then what?

They'd have him.

Take me, spirit.

There it was again. The voice. The whispers.

But I can't, Brennan thought. I can't go where I can't go, can't go, can't go . . .

Still he climbed the trail until he was moving across the flat, grassy meadow; moving now without purpose because he was sure he would not be able to get out of the cliffs that ringed the back of the canyon.

The sun cooked now, directly over the canyon. Even running—more jogging with a limp than running—he could not help but see the beauty of the canyon. The cliffs had looked red in the morning light but were now showing bars of gold and purple in the rock strata.

He saw the boulder now up ahead, where he had

found the skull, and for a moment he thought that was it—where he was supposed to go.

He thought that perhaps the skull wanted only that—to return to the place by the boulder to be with the rest of the skeleton, which must still be there.

But he knew he was wrong—something felt wrong about it.

What?

Not the boulder . . .

It was here—just so it was here. I ran, even with one leg I ran to reach the sky, reach the blue sky and freedom; ran to reach the medicine place but it was here, here that I ended. . . .

Brennan drew closer to the boulder. He had not known how it had been, and did not know it now. But he could feel something of it.

How the soldiers must have followed him—as the rescue men followed him now. Brennan hesitated as he neared the overhanging boulder, almost stopped and as he did the men gained on him, grew close enough so he could hear their feet.

No. Go on, go on and up and on to the place of medicine, to the ancient ones. . . .

There was great urgency in it, in the voice, in the feeling and he started to run again, past the boulder.

The sudden jump into a run twisted his sore leg and the limp grew temporarily worse and it slowed him. He could hear the men gaining again, their feet slamming into the dirt.

Ahead there was a ledge and a drop ten feet down into the streambed.

Brennan went off at a full trot and tumbled head over heels into the streambed in a cloud of dirt and loose rocks near the spring and pool of water. It looked cool, and inviting, but the streambed moved still farther up the canyon and he knew he had to continue.

The fall had knocked the wind out of him but he scrambled to his feet and started moving again, always up.

It looked worse all the time. The sides of the creek-bed grew steeper and higher and he could see no way to get out.

"You have taken me the wrong way," he said aloud between breaths.

But he kept moving. The streambed drew narrower still and began to wind sharply left and right and tighter and Brennan slowed, finally, thought it would end here.

Watch for a sign, the line of fire.

Ahh, he thought—sure. Watch for a sign. Fire? The line of fire?

And there it was, up and to the left.

In the wall of the streambed on the left side, about even with his forehead, there were several lines gouged in the rock. They were jagged and very old, faded and nearly gone and had he not been watching for them he would have missed them.

But he saw them and even as blurred as they were he knew they represented a bolt of lightning.

The line of fire.

Next to the blurred lightning bolt there was a fissure in the rock. It was narrow, went straight up the rock wall, and Brennan would have passed it, the way it lay back and partially out of sight, had he not been looking for the sign.

He looked back in the fissure—large crack in the cliff face, really—and saw two handholds just above his head, one on each side.

Up.

One word. He put his hands in the handholds and pulled himself up.

And there were two more.

And up, and two more, and still more and in twenty feet the fissure—which had been just wide enough for his body—began to widen and he saw that the handholds went on up the split in the rock all the way to the top of the canyon wall.

Three, four hundred feet.

Up.

Did he do this? Brennan felt the ridges with his fingers as he climbed, felt the edges where a tool had carved and chipped. They were weathered, old—very old. Ancient. Coyote Runs had not done this—the handholds had been there for hundreds, perhaps thousands of years.

But he had used them. Coyote Runs had used them. His hands and feet in the same place, pulling up.

Up.

Brennan kept climbing and when he was nearly fifty

feet up he paused and heard the two men come running up the rocky streambed. He held his breath—though they could never have heard him breathing—and the men ran past the fissure without pausing. Brennan smiled.

And it is so that I would have been free, been safe, if I had beaten them to the medicine steps. . . .

Brennan did some mental calculating. Maybe a quarter of a mile to the end of the canyon, perhaps a bit more.

Then they would start back. Ten, fifteen minutes. They would have to move slowly, looking for tracks, some sign of him in the rock streambed.

Maybe another ten, fifteen minutes. It was hard to estimate. Perhaps a total of twenty or thirty minutes until they found the fissure.

Then they would start up. They were expert climbers and would have no trouble.

Twenty minutes would have to be enough for whatever it was he was supposed to do.

He held for a moment, catching his breath and resting his legs, then he climbed again, looking up the fissure. The handholds were closer together now, made for a shorter body and it made the climbing faster, easier.

Above was the sky.

Blue sky. Not a cloud showed above in the narrow slot of the fissure. He climbed with his back to one side of the opening and his feet on the other, using the hand- and footholds on each side, and concentrated so hard on the climb that he didn't seem to notice how high he was getting until he nearly fell.

His hand slipped from one of the cutouts in his haste and had his foot not caught a hole on the other side and jammed him he would have dropped.

It was then, near the top, that he first looked outside the fissure and saw below him.

The canyon fell away beneath him in a drop that seemed to go forever. He could see out, past the mouth of the canyon, see the police and rescue cars there—they looked like toys—see the small specks that he knew to be his mother and the rest of them and his heart nearly froze.

He had never been this high, never climbed this way, and fear held him and he thought he would not be able to go on, to climb the short distance to the top.

Take me, spirit . . .

And his hand moved. He moved his eyes away from the view out of the fissure and looked only up. His hand found a new hole, then his feet and he skitched his back up, then a new handhold, then a foot, and up, and up and slowly he kept moving, kept climbing until he was at the top, until he could pull himself out on the flat rock of the top of the bluff where he lay for a moment, breathing deeply.

Then he stood.

And saw the world.

That was the only way he could think of it—he saw the world. The desert lay below him. He stood on a flat almost-table of rock that jutted out, formed one side of the canyon, and below and away lay all the world he knew. To his left, a haze in the south, lay El Paso, and across the great basin of desert he saw the Organ Mountains, gray and jagged, like broken teeth, and to his right, white and brilliant, lay the white sands, shining in the midday sun so bright it seemed the desert had been washed and bleached and painted.

And he saw this, Brennan thought.

He saw this same thing.

Coyote Runs was here, came up here, saw all this when he was still alive.

When he'd started the climb up the fissure he'd looped the handles of the knapsack around his neck so the pack with the skull would ride in front and be out of the way. He took it off now, let it hang in his hand.

To his right and perhaps twenty feet out on the flat rock was a squarish rock that seemed out of place. It was about a foot high and roughly two feet square, rounded by wind and weather at the edges, but Brennan's eyes were drawn to it.

The medicine place . . .

Of course, Brennan thought. Of course it is. . . .

He walked to the rock. In a small depression near it the limestone of the butte was a blackened color where there had obviously been fires.

Here it was, Brennan thought, here it was that he came to sit and learn things and know things. This was how he lived. How he was. Until they killed him.

The ancient ones are here, are always here in the medicine place. . . .

I understand, Brennan thought. He looked across the desert, stood by the rock and the small fire place and looked across the desert and understood why Coyote Runs had tried to get here, tried to be here, had brought him here finally in all the craziness of the run and the climb and the skull.

It was how he was, Brennan thought. It was the way of Coyote Runs to be here, to come here, to have his spirit set free here to go back to the ancient ones and he had been stopped, held back all these years, all this time.

Leave me, spirit . . .

Brennan nodded, smiled. He took the skull carefully from the knapsack and put it on the square rock, set it gently so the eyes were looking out at the desert and sky and moved away, stood away.

Be free, he thought, be the sun and wind and desert and stone and plant and the dust, be free and all the things there are to be.

He whispered, "Be free . . ."

And for a time there was nothing, for minutes or seconds or years there was nothing but the skull sitting on the rock and the world below.

Then a warm wind, a short, warm wind brushed his cheek and caught some dust from the rock around the skull and took the dust in a swirling column up, up over the bluff, over the canyon, over Brennan and into the sky and gone, gone where the dream of the eagle had flown, gone for all of time, gone and the skull was just that, a skull, a bone, nothing more, empty, as Brennan was empty.

He sighed, tears on his cheeks, missing something he did not understand, feeling that he had lost a friend somehow, and turned to meet the rescue men.

Gary Paulsen is the distinguished author of many critically acclaimed books for young people, including three Newbery Honor books, *The Winter Room, Hatchet,* and *Dogsong.* He lives with his wife and son in northern Minnesota.